"If You're Not Going To Let Me Seduce You, Then The Least You Can Do Is Dance With Me," Travis Said.

Eyes wide, Lacey let him pull her into his arms. "But there isn't any music!"

"Sure there is. Listen real close," he whispered in her ear.

Her cheek resting against his, she listened. "I don't hear anything."

"You're not concentrating hard enough," he scolded. "Close your eyes."

Dutifully Lacey did as he instructed.

"Feel that?" He flattened his hand against her back and pressed her close to his chest. "That's my heart beating for you."

The music flowed through Lacey like wine, warming her blood. She stared up at him. "Yes," she murmured. "I can hear it." She watched his eyes darken. Then his face was lowering to hers.

"I *am* going to seduce you," he warned.

"Too late," she whispered as his lips touched hers. "You already have."

Dear Reader,

Please join us in celebrating Silhouette's 20th anniversary in 2000! We promise to deliver—all year—passionate, powerful, provocative love stories from your favorite Desire authors!

This January, look for bestselling author Leanne Banks's first MAN OF THE MONTH with *Her Forever Man*. Watch sparks fly when irresistibly rugged ranch owner Brock Logan comes face-to-face with his new partner, the fiery Felicity Chambeau, in the first book of Leanne's brand-new miniseries LONE STAR FAMILIES: THE LOGANS.

Desire is pleased to continue the Silhouette cross-line continuity ROYALLY WED with *The Pregnant Princess* by favorite author Anne Marie Winston. After a night of torrid passion with a stranger, a beautiful princess ends up pregnant...and seeks out the father of her child.

Elizabeth Bevarly returns to Desire with her immensely popular miniseries FROM HERE TO MATERNITY with *Dr. Mommy,* about a couple reunited by a baby left on a doorstep. *Hard Lovin' Man,* another of Peggy Moreland's TEXAS BRIDES, captures the intensity of falling in love when a cowgirl gives her heart to a sweet-talkin', hard-lovin' hunk. Cathleen Galitz delivers a compelling marriage-of-convenience tale in *The Cowboy Takes a Bride,* in the series THE BRIDAL BID. And Sheri WhiteFeather offers another provocative Native American hero in *Skyler Hawk: Lone Brave.*

Help us celebrate 20 years of great romantic fiction from Silhouette by indulging yourself with all six delectably sensual Desire titles each and every month during this special year!

Enjoy!

Joan Marlow Golan
Senior Editor, Silhouette Desire

Please address questions and book requests to:
Silhouette Reader Service
U.S.: 3010 Walden Ave., P.O. Box 1325, Buffalo, NY 14269
Canadian: P.O. Box 609, Fort Erie, Ont. L2A 5X3

Hard Lovin' Man

PEGGY MORELAND

Published by Silhouette Books

America's Publisher of Contemporary Romance

Life is full of disappointments, some stemming from
circumstances beyond our control. To all who have
suffered but managed to find the rainbow after the
storm, joy in the simple things, love when least
expected…this book is for you.

 SILHOUETTE BOOKS

ISBN 0-373-76270-4

HARD LOVIN' MAN

Copyright © 2000 by Peggy Bozeman Morse

This edition published by arrangement with Harlequin Books S.A.

® and TM are trademarks of Harlequin Books S.A., used under license.
Trademarks indicated with ® are registered in the United States Patent
and Trademark Office, the Canadian Trade Marks Office and in other
countries.

Visit us at www.romance.net

Printed in U.S.A.

PEGGY MORELAND

published her first romance with Silhouette in 1989.
She's a natural storyteller with a sense of humor that will
tickle your fancy, and Peggy's goal is to write a story that
readers will remember long after the last page is turned.
Winner of the 1992 National Readers' Choice Award,
and a 1994 RITA finalist, Peggy frequently appears on
bestseller lists around the country. A native Texan, she
and her family live in Round Rock, Texas.

IT'S OUR 20th ANNIVERSARY!
We'll be celebrating all year, starting with these fabulous titles, on sale in January 2000.

Special Edition

#1297 Matt Caldwell: Texas Tycoon
Diana Palmer

#1298 Their Little Princess
Susan Mallery

#1299 The Baby Legacy
Pamela Toth

#1300 Summer Hawk
Peggy Webb

#1301 Daddy by Surprise
Pat Warren

#1302 Lonesome No More
Jean Brashear

Intimate Moments

#979 Murdock's Last Stand
Beverly Barton

#980 Marrying Mike... Again
Alicia Scott

#981 A Drive-By Wedding
Terese Ramin

#982 Midnight Promises
Eileen Wilks

#983 The Comeback of Con MacNeill
Virginia Kantra

#984 Witness... and Wife?
Kate Stevenson

Romance

 #1420 The Baby Bequest
Susan Meier

#1421 With a Little T.L.C.
Teresa Southwick

#1422 The Sheik's Solution
Barbara McMahon

 #1423 Annie and the Prince
Elizabeth Harbison

#1424 A Babe in the Woods
Cara Colter

#1425 Prim, Proper... Pregnant
Alice Sharpe

Desire

 #1267 Her Forever Man
Leanne Banks

 #1268 The Pregnant Princess
Anne Marie Winston

 #1269 Dr. Mommy
Elizabeth Bevarly

 **#1270 Hard Lovin' Man**
Peggy Moreland

#1271 The Cowboy Takes a Bride
Cathleen Galitz

#1272 Skyler Hawk: Lone Brave
Sheri WhiteFeather

One

Double-Cross Heart Ranch.

Frowning, Lacey looped an arm around the steering wheel and leaned forward to peer through the windshield at the wrought-iron sign hanging above the ranch's entrance. Fitting, she decided bitterly. In her estimation, the owner of the ranch—Lucas McCloud—was a double-crossing, heart-breaking, low-crawling snake, so it seemed only appropriate that his ranch's name would reflect those same traits.

And today she planned to tell him face-to-face what a lowlife she thought he was. Firming her lips in determination, she made the turn into the ranch's entrance and bumped her way across the cattle guard.

Cattle grazed along both sides of the long drive, unaffected by the dust she stirred, but a small herd of horses lifted their heads as she passed by, curious. Another time, another place, she might have stopped just to enjoy the beauty of the animals and the rugged Texas landscape. But not today. Today she was on a mission.

She'd waited two years for this moment. The rodeo in Fort Worth the night before had put her in close enough proximity to Austin and the Double-Cross Heart Ranch to justify the trip. Not that she needed justification. To her way of thinking, a confrontation with Lucas McCloud was long overdue.

As she topped a small rise, a sprawling ranch house popped into view—and, without warning, butterflies the size of bats took wing in her stomach. She pressed a hand to her middle, and tried to swallow back the unexpected attack of nerves. She could do this, she reminded herself firmly. And once she'd had her say, she was hightailing it back to Missouri, and she'd never have to so much as *think* the man's name again.

Parking her truck in front of the house, she hopped down and marched to the porch. She rapped her knuckles hard against the thick oak door then stepped back and folded her arms across her chest, waiting.

She had just about decided to knock again when the door opened and a harried young woman appeared. But before Lacey could state her business, someone inside the house shouted, "Mandy! Where's the Bible?"

The woman called over her shoulder, "In the bookcase in the office," then rolled her eyes as she turned back to Lacey. She offered an apologetic smile. "Sorry. Things are a little crazy around here at the moment. We're getting ready for a wedding."

A wedding? As usual Lacey's timing sucked wind. Didn't matter, though, she told herself. Wedding, or not, she was staying until she'd seen Lucas McCloud and said her piece.

The woman extended a hand in greeting, her smile

growing warmer. "I'm Mandy Barrister. What can I do for you?"

Reluctantly, Lacey unfolded her arms and shook the offered hand. "Lacey Cline. I'm here to see Lucas McCloud."

"Lucas?" the woman repeated, her smile slowly fading.

"Yeah," Lacey replied, not bothering to hide the bitterness in her tone. "Tell him his *daughter* is here to see him."

The woman grabbed for the doorframe, her eyes going wide. "*You're* Lucas's daughter?"

Ignoring the question, Lacey leaned to peer around her. "Is he here? I'm in kind of a hurry."

Drawing in a long breath, the woman uncurled her fingers from the doorframe and straightened, lifting her hand helplessly. "No. He's—" She dropped the hand limply to her side. "Lucas is dead."

A hoof with fifteen hundred pounds of horsepower behind it could have hit the wall of Lacey's chest and had a lesser effect on her ability to breathe. "Dead?" she managed to choke out.

"Yes. For about thirteen years now."

Lucas was dead? Lacey raked her fingers through her hair, trying to get a grip on her spinning emotions. She'd waited two years for the opportunity to tell the man who had sired her what a low-crawling snake she thought he was for refusing to acknowledge her as his daughter. She supposed she should be glad he was dead...but for some reason, all she felt was a huge gaping hole in her chest. She backed up a step. "I—I'm sorry," she stammered, then, unable to think of anything else to say, turned and ran down the steps.

She'd almost made it to her truck when she heard footsteps running behind her.

"Lacey! Wait!"

She stopped, drawing in a deep breath before turning. The distress she saw on the woman's face shamed her. She didn't know what kind of memories her request to see Lucas had stirred, but obviously they weren't pleasant ones. "Listen...Mandy, isn't it?" At the woman's nod, she hurried on. "Look, Mandy, I'm sorry I bothered you. I didn't know."

"You said you were Lucas's daughter."

"Yeah," she mumbled, and dropped her gaze to hide the unwanted tears that swelled again.

"So am I."

Lacey's head shot up. "What did you say?"

Mandy drew in a shuddery breath. "I'm Lucas's daughter. I have two younger sisters, Merideth and Sam."

Lucas had daughters? Then that meant Lacey had half sisters. Numbed by the realization, she stared, speechless.

Mandy seemed at a loss for words, too, because she clasped her hands together and squeezed until her knuckles looked like a string of pearls wrapped around her fists, before she lifted her hands in a helpless shrug. "I—I don't know what to say to you."

Lacey clamped her lips together in a frown. "You don't have to say anything. Like I said, I'm sorry." She turned away again, but Mandy grabbed her arm, stopping her.

"Please don't go," she begged. She glanced toward the house, catching her lower lip between her teeth. "We've got this wedding," she began hesitantly, then turned to Lacey again. "But it shouldn't last too long, and I really would like to talk to you. We all would."

Lacey eased from the woman's grasp, regretting that she'd ever stepped foot on the Double-Cross. "Sorry, but

I came to talk to Lucas. Since he's dead, there's no reason for me to hang around.''

"But Sam and Merideth will want to meet you.''

Lacey snorted a laugh. "I doubt that.''

Mandy scowled, obviously irritated by Lacey's sarcasm. "Well, I don't, and I think I would know their preferences better than you.''

Lacey moved her shoulder in a shrug. "Can't argue that, since I didn't even know they existed, or you, either, for that matter, until a couple of minutes ago.''

Mandy lifted her chin defensively. "Well, we didn't know you existed, either, until you showed up on our doorstep.''

Aware that the conversation was going nowhere fast, Lacey tried to think of a way to end it. "Look," she said, fighting for patience. "Just pretend I was never here, and that this conversation never took place. Okay?''

"No way.'' Pursing her lips, Mandy grabbed Lacey's hand and dragged her toward the house. "You can't expect to drop a bomb like that and just drive away, leaving us with a thousand unanswered questions.''

Lacey dug in her boot heels, trying to wrench free, but was surprised to discover that, though the woman appeared delicate, her strength equaled Lacey's own. "Hey! I said I was sorry. Okay? It was a mistake. I should never have come here.''

"Too late," Mandy muttered.

"But you're getting ready for a wedding," Lacey reminded her, grasping at straws, anything to escape. "Your cousin Alayna's wedding. You'll want to meet her, too.''

Lacey jerked to a stop and succeeded in dragging Mandy to a stop, as well. Half sisters *and* cousins? She'd never thought about Lucas having a family. He'd been just a name to her, not a real person...and she wanted no part of his family. "My horse is in the trailer," she said on sudden inspiration. "I can't leave him there in this heat."

Mandy gave Lacey's hand another jerk, hauling her up the steps behind her. "Don't worry. I'll have my son Jaime take care of him for you."

She opened the door and all but shoved Lacey inside ahead of her. "Merideth! Sam!" she called. "Come here. I've got someone I want you to meet."

Lacey stood at the back of the cavernous living room, trying her best to melt into the wall. The room was crowded with members of the McCloud family—all of them strangers to her. Half sisters. Brothers-in-law. Cousins. Nieces and nephews. Before the wedding had started, Mandy had insisted on introducing her to every last one.

She drew in a shaky breath. She still wasn't sure how Mandy had managed to rope her into staying for the ceremony. She didn't want to be here. She wanted to be on the road, headed for Missouri, and as far away from the Double-Cross Heart Ranch as she could get.

But she wasn't. And it didn't look as if she was going to be able to leave any time soon.

The hair on the back of her neck prickled, and she angled her head slightly to find Merideth staring at her, a slight frown curving her lips. Lacey frowned right back. With a haughty lift of her chin, Merideth turned away, centering her attention on the preacher and the bride and groom who stood in front of the massive fireplace.

To heck with you, Lacey fumed silently, forcing her gaze to the ceremony. She wasn't here to win any friends. Heck, she didn't even know *why* she was here!

Well, she did know, she reflected morosely as the

preacher's voice droned on and on as he read a long passage from the Bible. It was all Mandy's doing. There had only been enough time for quick introductions before the wedding had started, and Mandy had insisted that Lacey stay until after the ceremony when they would have more time to talk. Lacey had finally agreed, just to get the spotlight off her for a while. Being introduced as Lucas's illegitimate daughter and having all those people staring at her had been a little disconcerting.

She had to give it to them, though, she thought with a sigh. To their credit, not a one of them had questioned her claim as Lucas's daughter, and all had treated her civilly.

Other than Merideth, of course.

Lacey glanced Merideth's way again, frowning at the back of her blond head. It wasn't that Merideth had been rude exactly. She just kept watching Lacey as if she expected to catch her slipping off with the family silver or something.

Lacey pursed her mouth in irritation and turned her gaze back to the front of the room. Discovering one of her half sisters was a movie star had come as a shock, but hadn't changed Lacey's feelings toward Meredith. She didn't care for Meredith any more than Meredith cared for her, movie star or not. And as soon as this hitching was over, she told herself, she was getting out of here, promise or not. She didn't owe the McClouds any explanations, and as far as she was concerned, they didn't owe her any, either.

She heard the front door open behind her and glanced over her shoulder to see who was arriving late. She choked back a laugh when she realized the futility in that gesture. She didn't know the bride and groom, much less any of their wedding guests. With a shake of her head, she turned her attention back to the ceremony, silently praying that the long-winded preacher would speed things up.

She felt a shoulder bump hers and glanced over to find a man had slipped into the room and was standing beside her. When she got a good look at his face, she did a quick double take, snapping her gaze to the front of the room and the groom, then back to the man at her side, sure that she was hallucinating. The two men could be identical twins—only the groom was wearing a suit, and the man beside her was wearing camouflage pants and a black T-shirt. She smothered a laugh. And she'd been concerned about attending the ceremony dressed in boots and jeans.

The eyes that met hers were a deep chocolate brown, and she couldn't help but stare. His face obviously hadn't seen a razor in a couple of days, because the stubbled beginnings of a mustache and beard the same shade of brown as the hair that brushed the neck of his black T-shirt covered his jaw and chin. And his eyes. There was a wildness, a desperation in them that was downright scary.

"Sorry," he mumbled, and shifted away, putting space between them.

Tearing her gaze from his, Lacey quickly turned her attention back to the ceremony just as the minister said, "If anyone present knows of a reason why this man and this woman should not be joined in holy matrimony, may he speak now or forever hold his peace."

"I do!" the man beside her growled.

Lacey whipped her head around to stare at him, as did everyone else in the room. As Lacey had, to a person, they did a double take when they got their first look at his face.

"Travis!" the groom exclaimed, a smile beginning to spread over his face. "You came!"

The stranger—Travis, the groom had called him—didn't return the smile. "And just in the nick of time," Lacey heard him mutter under his breath as he pushed himself away from the wall. He took a step forward, then stopped, squaring shoulders as broad as those of the man he confronted. "Mike, our foreman, sent me a wire relaying your message. I can't let you go through with this, Jack."

The smile that had bloomed on the groom's face quickly dipped into a scowl. He turned back to the preacher. "Ignore him. Go on with the ceremony."

Travis took another step forward. "Don't listen to him, preacher. He's crazy."

Lacey watched the groom's shoulders rise then fall in an obvious search for patience before he turned slowly back around. "There's nothing wrong with me, Travis. I'm okay now."

Travis closed the distance between them. "No, you're not." He nodded his head toward Alayna, who was staring at him, her eyes wide with shock, her face pale beneath the sheer veil that shadowed her face. "Not if you're about to get married again. You made one mistake. I can't stand by and watch you make another."

"Then leave," the groom snapped. He turned to face the preacher again. "Finish the job," he growled.

The preacher gulped, glancing nervously from one man to the other.

Travis slapped a hand on Jack's shoulder and whipped him around to face him. "If I leave," he said, the warning undergirded with a thick layer of steel, "I'm taking you with me."

Jack's face turned bloodred with rage. He knocked Travis's hand from his shoulder. "Like hell you are."

If asked later, Lacey couldn't have said who threw the first punch, but, in the blink of an eye, fists were flying. The bride screamed and one of the little kids in the room started crying. Another kid yelled, "Cool, dude! Hit him again, Dad!"

There was a grunt of pain, but Lacey couldn't be sure if it was Travis or Jack who had made the guttural sound.

Mandy's husband, Jesse, and Sam's husband, Nash, quickly jumped into the fray, trying to pull Jack and Travis apart. But it was Merideth's husband John Lee—a tall man with arms as thick as his wife's waist—who managed to wedge himself between the two men and separate them. For his trouble, he caught the left meant for Jack square on the chin.

Testing his jaw to make sure it wasn't broken, John Lee kept a hand braced on Jack's chest, holding him back, while Jesse and Nash struggled to pen Travis's arms behind his back.

John Lee looked from one furious face to the other, then suggested mildly, "Now why don't you boys tell the rest of us what this little scuffle's all about."

"He's crazy," the two men said in unison, gesturing with their chins at the other.

John Lee nodded his head. "Well, I'd have to agree with you on that score, because you're both acting like a couple of nutcases." He glanced over at Travis. "Nice left," he added, rubbing his still-throbbing chin.

"Thanks," Travis grumbled.

Lacey would've laughed at the absurdity of the conversation, but she was afraid she might miss something.

John Lee let his hand drop from Jack's chest and began to pace between the two men, his hands clasped behind his back, looking much like a trial lawyer preparing to question a crucial witness. He stopped after a moment to peer at Travis. "So why'd you want to stop the wedding?"

Travis scowled at Jack. "Because he's not ready to get married."

"That's a damn lie."

John Lee made a tsking sound with his tongue. "Now, Jack," he scolded gently. "Remember there are ladies and children present, not to mention a man of the cloth."

Jack stuffed his hands in his pockets and ducked his head, properly chastised. "Sorry," he mumbled, then shifted his gaze to Travis's, his eyes narrowing dangerously. "I know what I'm doing."

Travis shook his head. "You may *think* you do, but you're still running on emotion. Your wife's been dead less than a year."

"*Ex*-wife," Jack corrected.

John Lee listened to the exchange, then focused on Jack. "Do you love Alayna?"

"With all my heart."

"And you want to marry her?"

Jack turned to his bride and took her hand, squeezing it in his own as he gazed deeply into her eyes. "Yes."

"And do you want to marry Jack?" he asked the bride.

Her lips trembling uncontrollably, she could only nod her head.

John Lee lifted a shoulder. "That's good enough for me." He turned to Travis. "I'd say you're fighting a losing battle, buddy." He eyed him a moment longer. "Think you can behave yourself, now?"

"Yeah," Travis muttered, though Lacey could see that there was still some fight left in him.

John Lee gave a nod to Jesse and Nash. "Turn him loose."

Scowling, Travis jerked free of the two men, then dragged the back of his wrist across his mouth, swiping a trickle of blood from a lip that was quickly swelling. John Lee pulled a handkerchief from his pocket and offered it to him.

"Thanks," Travis mumbled.

John Lee folded his arms across his chest and reared back to study him. "Judging by the resemblance, I'd say you'd have to be Jack's twin."

Travis shot his brother a glare, then turned to John Lee, sighing heavily as he stretched a hand out in greeting. "Yeah. Travis Cordell."

John Lee smiled as he shook the offered hand. "Pleased to meet you, Travis. I'm John Lee Carter." He leaned close. "Do you mind if I ask you a question?"

Self-consciously, Travis lifted a shoulder. "No, I guess not."

"Do y'all always scrap like this?"

The brothers exchanged an indefinable look, then Travis mumbled, "Yeah. Mostly."

John Lee chuckled and slapped a companionable arm around Travis's shoulder. "That's what I figured." He turned Travis toward the door. "How about you and me go and grab us a beer and let these folks get on with their business?"

Though the wedding had proved to be more entertaining than Lacey had expected, she wasn't sure how much more of this family-ness she could take. With the reception now in full swing and Mandy busy playing hostess, Lacey's patience was quickly wearing thin as she waited for the promised meeting with her half sisters. She

couldn't count the number of toasts that had been made
to the newlyweds, or how many times a camera flash had
gone off in her face. She quickly stepped out of the path
of a pair of towheaded kids, squealing and laughing while
they played a game of chase through the crowd of well-
wishers.

With a sigh, she glanced around in hopes of catching
Mandy's eye, but instead her gaze settled on the groom's
brother, who stood on the fringe of the festivities. She
couldn't help but feel sorry for him. Though she couldn't
agree with his methods, she figured his heart had been in
the right place when he'd tried to stop the wedding. And
at the moment, he looked as if he felt as out-of-place and
miserable as she did. Sensing a kinship of sorts, she
moved to stand beside him.

"How's the lip?"

He lifted the ice pack he held at the corner of his mouth
and muttered, "It hurts," then replaced it.

Lacey stepped in front of him, squinting her eyes to
better see his face in the glow from the torches lining the
fan-shaped patio. "That eye looks pretty bad, too. Have
you put anything on it?"

He puckered his brow, obviously unaware of the injury,
and lifted a hand to inspect it. He flinched when his fingers grazed the raw flesh.

She bit back a grin. "I guess you haven't." She glanced
toward the house, wondering if she could find a first-aid
kit in the kitchen, then shuddered when she saw the sea
of people she'd have to wade through in order to reach
the back door. Squaring her shoulders, she hooked her
arm through his. "Come on, killer. I've got some horse
liniment in my trailer."

"Horse liniment!" he cried, jerking her to a stop. "I'm
no horse."

She chuckled and gave him a tug, all but dragging him toward the barn where her truck and trailer were now parked. "No, but judging by the show you put on earlier, you could be a distant relation. A jackass," she explained at his questioning look.

He snorted, then winced at the pain the action caused him.

Chuckling, she slipped her arm from his and opened the side door that led to the trailer's sleeping quarters. She stepped inside, pausing to flip on a light. Moving easily in the confined space, she opened a cabinet door and pulled down a first-aid kit. When she saw that Travis still stood outside, watching her warily, she gestured for him to join her. "It's okay, killer," she said, holding up the box. "I've got medications for humans, too."

Reluctantly he climbed inside. She waved him toward a wide, padded bench that she hoped to someday convert into a bed for use when she was traveling the rodeo circuit. "Have a seat and I'll take a look."

He dropped down, his look guarded as he watched her flip open the box and remove a packet.

"Pre-soaked antiseptic gauze," she said, responding to the suspicion in his eyes.

When she tried to apply the gauze to the cut, he reared his head back and grabbed her wrist, stopping her. "You hurt me," he warned, meeting her gaze, "and I'll have to hurt you back."

The strength in his hand surprised her, but it was the emotion in his brown eyes that had the breath backing up in her lungs. Anger, frustration, concern. They all churned there, but it was his concern—a concern she instinctively attributed to his lingering worry over his brother's marriage—that squeezed at her heart. Hoping to distill the sympathy she felt building, she teased, "Sissy."

His scowl deepened, but he loosened his grip on her hand.

Mindful of his warning, though she sensed he wasn't the kind of man who would make good the threat, she kept her touch gentle as she dabbed the gauze at the cut, cleaning it. "That brother of yours has a mean right hook."

"Lucky punch," he muttered disagreeably.

She bit back a smile. "Maybe," she conceded, and continued to cleanse the wound. "Was it really worth all this to try to stop his wedding?"

"It would've been if I'd succeeded."

"You said he was crazy."

"Poor choice of words."

"What is he, then?"

"Confused. Grieving." He sighed heavily. "He lost his son and his ex-wife in an automobile accident less than a year ago. He's been on the run ever since."

"Tough break."

"Yeah, you could say that."

"So you think he's marrying on the rebound?"

"It's a possibility. A strong one."

"He sounded sincere enough to me."

"Maybe," he said doubtfully.

With a shrug of apparent indifference, Lacey tossed aside the strip of gauze and picked up another.

Travis watched her, frowning, wishing he shared her detachment. But he didn't. Jack was his brother. His twin brother. And when Jack hurt, so did he. Jack's first marriage had left scars that Travis felt partially responsible for, and the accident that had stolen his son had left his brother—in Travis's opinion—emotionally unstable. As a result, he felt duty-bound to see that his brother wasn't hurt again.

He sighed heavily, feeling the frustration building. He didn't want to think about his brother's current emotional state any more, or his own failure to stop the wedding.

And the woman who was nursing his cuts offered just the distraction he needed to forget his troubles for awhile. A tight little butt, small waist, full ripe breasts. Sensuous lips pursed in concentration.

His own lips began to curve upward as she moved to stand between his spread knees again. Yeah, she was just the distraction he needed. Pleased with his current situation, he laid his head back and closed his eyes, prepared to enjoy the feminine attention. He felt her fingers graze his temple as she combed back his hair, then the weight of her hand when she pressed her palm against the side of his head, holding his hair out of her way. Soothed by her touch, he inhaled deeply...and filled his senses with her. No flowery perfumes for this woman, he reflected, fully relaxed now. Just soap, sunshine and pure woman.

Intrigued by her and by the brief story John Lee had shared with him about her questionable ancestry, he opened his eyes to study her. The light was behind her and left shadows on her face, but he could see well enough to make out her features. Wide green eyes framed by long dark lashes, a cute button of a nose with a light sprinkling of freckles across its bridge. Full sensuous lips, a stubborn chin.

A face full of contradictions.

As he decided this, she placed a finger beneath his chin and angled his face toward the light, furrowing her forehead in concern.

"That cut's pretty deep," she said uneasily. "You might need a couple of stitches."

"Can you sew?"

Startled by the question, she shifted her gaze to his.

"No," she said, then bit back a smile when she saw that he was teasing. She glanced at the cut again and sighed, shaking her head. "But without stitches, you're going to have a scar."

"It'll just add character."

She shrugged as she straightened. "It's your face."

"And a handsome one, huh?"

She snorted a laugh and tossed aside the square of soiled cotton. "Watch it. Your ego's showing."

He caught her hand, and pulled her back around to face him. "Are you a nurse?"

Standing so close, Lacey had to admit that he was right. He did have a handsome face. And, fat lip or not, the sexiest smile she believed she'd ever seen.

Uncomfortably aware of the hand that held hers, she eased free and reached for the antiseptic cream. "No. I'm a barrel racer." She squeezed a dollop of cream onto her finger and leaned to smear it on the cut.

"A barrel racer, huh? Too bad. You'd have made a good nurse. You've got a nice touch."

Not knowing what to say in reply, she remained silent as she dabbed the cream along the wound.

"You're Lacey, right?"

"Uh-huh."

"I'd have guessed right off."

"Guessed what?" she asked absently, concentrating on keeping the cream on the cut and out of his eye.

"That you're a McCloud."

She jerked her hand away and straightened, staring down at him. "How?"

"You look just like 'em."

Frowning, she tore her gaze from his and grabbed a rag to wipe the cream from her fingers. "No, I don't."

When he laughed, she shot him a look sharp enough to fillet a fish…but he just smiled. "Sorry, but you do."

"I do not," she repeated firmly.

"Yeah, you do." When she huffed a breath, he laughed again. "I didn't mean that as an insult. Hell, they're all beautiful women." He watched her rip open a bandage, her jerky movements reflecting her agitation, and added, "But I guess, being a woman, you wouldn't have noticed that." Her scowl deepened as she leaned to place the bandage over the cut. "Now, take me for instance—" he began, then flinched when she pressed the bandage into place.

"Sorry," she mumbled.

"No harm done," he said and continued with his observation. "I noticed right off how pretty they were, and I knew immediately that they were sisters."

"How? They don't look a thing alike."

"Their colorings different, and they're built differently, but the similarities are there."

Having completed her first aid, she gave him a nudge with her hip, making room for herself on the bench, then dropped down beside him. Pulling the kit to her lap, she started replacing the supplies. "Enlighten me."

"The way they walk, the way they talk. They're all three strong women, sure of themselves and each other and their place in the family unit."

Lacey snorted and closed the lid with a snap. "Well, if that's what you're basing your assessment on, you're wrong, because I don't have a place in this family."

"Yeah, you do." He grinned when she turned to glare at him. "You just haven't found it, yet."

"Yeah, right," she muttered and stood, stretching to replace the kit in the cabinet.

Travis watched her, noticing the way her shirt molded

those firm breasts, the tiny waist, the slender hips, the long stretch of muscular legs. He appreciated a beautiful woman, always had, and he considered the one he was currently looking at a prime example of the gender.

Deciding the trip to the Double-Cross might not be a total loss after all, he smiled as he took advantage of her precarious position and bumped his foot against her left boot, knocking her off-balance. She sucked in a startled breath, flailing her arms in an attempt to recover...but dropped neatly into his lap, just as he'd planned.

He wrapped his arms around her waist from behind and snugged her back against his chest, nuzzling his nose in her hair. "Is this a bed I'm sitting on?" he whispered at her ear.

She held her body rigid against his. "Y-yes."

"Is it big enough for two to lie down on?"

"N-no."

"That's okay," he said, and nipped playfully at her earlobe, "'cause I was kinda hoping you'd be stretched out on top of me, anyway."

Two

Lacey wasn't sure who she was madder at. Travis for making a pass at her, or herself for being tempted by it.

She quickly decided it was Travis who deserved her anger.

"Of all the nerve," she muttered darkly as she stalked down the long hall in search of Mandy. Imagine him making a move like that, and after she'd been nice enough to doctor his wounds for him, too. And he'd called his brother crazy. She snorted in disgust. In her opinion, *Travis* was the one with the mental problem.

She stopped at the door one of the guests had directed her to, and drew in a deep breath, forcing herself to calm down before she stepped inside for the long-awaited meeting with her half sisters.

Mandy rose with a sigh of relief from behind a massive desk. "I was afraid you'd given up on us and left."

Feigning nonchalance, Lacey lifted a shoulder. "Thought

about it.'' Out of the corner of her eye, she caught a
movement and glanced over to find Merideth and Sam
sitting on the couch. Sam smiled at her. Merideth, her lips
pursed in displeasure, merely lifted a neatly arched brow.

Mandy gestured toward a wingback chair placed at an
angle to both the sofa and the desk. ''Please, have a seat.''

Feeling much like she had at the age of twelve when
she'd been called to the principal's office for putting a
frog in Elizabeth Conners's lunchbox, Lacey dropped
down onto the edge of the chair and wiped damp palms
down her thighs.

Mandy sat too. ''I apologize for the delay, but—'' She
laughed and sank wearily against the chair's back, lacing
her fingers over her abdomen. ''It's been rather an unusual
day.''

''You can say that again,'' Lacey replied dryly.

''Why don't you tell us about yourself,'' Mandy suggested, offering a warm smile of encouragement.

''You mean, about my relationship to Lucas?''

''Well, yes,'' Mandy said and shrugged self-
consciously. ''Naturally, we have a few questions.''

''I doubt I have any answers.''

With a humph, Merideth folded her arms across her
breasts. ''Some proof that you're Lucas's daughter would
be nice.''

''Merideth!'' Sam and Mandy exclaimed, mortified by
her rudeness.

Their sister flung out an arm, sending the gold bangles
on her wrist clinking musically as she gestured toward
Lacey. ''Well, how do you know she isn't some scam
artist who's trying to steal a piece of the Double-Cross?''

Mandy gave Merideth a quelling look before turning to
Lacey, her expression softening with regret. ''I'm sorry,

but surely you must realize how difficult this is for us all.''

Though Merideth's comment had stung, Lacey fought back the resentment, knowing that of all the reactions her claim to be Lucas's daughter had drawn, Merideth's was the most logical. ''No apology necessary. I'd probably want the same, if I were in y'all's position.'' She lifted her hands, palms up. ''But I don't have the proof you want. Only what my mother told me.''

Mandy leaned forward, resting her forearms on the desk. ''And what was that?''

''Just that she met Lucas at a horse show when she was nineteen. I don't know how old he would've been at the time, but I'm twenty-three, so you can do the math. They had an affair. A brief one. I was the by-product,'' she added bitterly.

Though she would have liked nothing better than to end the explanation there, she took a deep breath and forced herself to go on, hoping that once they heard it all, they would allow her to leave in peace. ''When my mother discovered she was pregnant, she contacted Lucas and de-manded that he marry her. He refused. My mother had been dating another man off and on for a while, both before and after Lucas, and he agreed to marry her in-stead. I didn't know until my twenty-first birthday that the man she'd married wasn't my father.''

As she listened, Mandy puckered her brow in confu-sion. ''Why did your mother wait until you were twenty-one to tell you the truth of your parentage?''

''She probably wouldn't have told me then, but she had no other choice.'' She sat up straighter, refusing to let the pain of Lucas's rejection show. ''Lucas didn't want me, but he set up a trust fund for me that became mine on my twenty-first birthday.''

"You've known for two years that Lucas was your father?"

Lacey glanced at Sam, who had asked the question, and slowly nodded.

"So why did you wait until *now* to come here?" Merideth snapped peevishly.

Lacey narrowed an eye as she shifted her gaze to Merideth's. "It took me that long to get past the hate."

Silence hummed in the room for a full thirty seconds as the two women engaged in a stubborn staring match. Lacey was the one to break it. She turned to Mandy, her eyes darkened in anger. "My turn to ask a question. Why is it that no one, other than her," she said, with a jerk of her head in Merideth's direction, "seems to doubt my claim to be Lucas's daughter?"

"I don't doubt your claim," Merideth cut in. "It's your motive that I question."

Lacey was on her feet, her eyes blazing, before Mandy or Sam could chastise their sister again for her rudeness. "If you think I'm here to claim a part of this ranch, you're wrong." She jammed a hand in her pocket, jerked out a folded piece of paper and slapped it on the desk in front of Mandy. "That's my check for the twenty-five thousand Lucas put in trust for me, plus the interest it earned over the years. My only purpose in coming here today was to shove it down his throat and tell him I don't need him *or* his money."

Mandy rose, her eyes filled with compassion. "Oh, Lacey. I'm so sorry. Lucas was a—"

"Mom!" Jaime, Mandy's son, burst into the room, his face pale, his eyes wide with fear. "Come quick. Billy fell off the top bunk and he's bleeding really bad."

Sam and Merideth jumped up and ran for the door, followed quickly by Jaime. Mandy snatched up the check and rounded the desk. She stopped in front of Lacey and grabbed her hand, pressing the check into it. "This is yours."

Fighting back tears, Lacey tried to pull free. "I don't want Lucas's money or anything else that was his."

Mandy forced Lacey's fingers to curl around the check. "Believe me. I understand how you feel. But Lucas owes you a lot more than this."

"Mom!" Jaime yelled from the hallway. "Hurry!"

Mandy squeezed Lacey's fist between her hands. "God, I'm sorry to keep doing this to you, but Billy is one of Alayna and Jack's children and our responsibility while they're on their honeymoon. If you could wait for just a little while longer."

Then she was gone, leaving Lacey alone in the office.

Lacey drew in a shaky breath as she continued to stare at her fist, still able to feel the warmth and compassion of Mandy's hands around it. Her sister. *Half* sister, she corrected. She let her head loll back, closing her eyes as emotion rose to burn her throat.

Oh, God, she'd always wanted a sister, the support and love of a caring family. But why did she have to find it here, in the home of the man who had rejected her?

Gulping back the sob that threatened, she forced her eyes open…and found herself looking straight into the eyes of Lucas McCloud.

She knew it was Lucas in the portrait, though there was nothing that identified the man as such. The eyes that stared back at her were the same green as her own, the same green as Mandy's. But the artist had captured a hardness, a coldness in his eyes that was lacking in Mandy's…and she hoped in hers. Drawn by her first glimpse of the man who had sired her, she moved closer to the portrait.

He sat astride a stallion, black as midnight, who stood on the edge of a high cliff. Blue sky surrounded them, and nothing but sheer rock lay below. There was an arrogance, a wildness about both horse and rider, that she could almost feel. A shiver chased down her spine as she stared unblinking at the man who had shunned her.

She could see why her mother had given herself to him. He was handsome, dangerously so, and projected an image as big as the state he called home. She felt the tears burn in her throat, behind her eyes, in her nose. He'd rejected his own daughter without even knowing her, refused to give her his name when he knew full well that she was of his blood. Her fingers curled, crumpling the check within her clenched fist.

"Bastard," she whispered. She threw the balled paper onto the desk and whirled, turning her back on Lucas McCloud as he had on her so many years before.

Mandy picked up the wad of paper from the desk and smoothed it open over her palm. "She's gone," she said, her voice heavy with regret as she lifted her gaze to look at her sisters. "And she left the check."

Merideth caught her lower lip between her teeth. "It's my fault. I was rude. Cruel."

Sam slung an arm around her shoulders. "Nah, you were just being you."

Merideth whipped her head around and gave Sam a scathing look. Chuckling, Sam hugged her younger sister to her side. "Ah, come on, Sis. You know you're our balance. If left up to Mandy, we'd already be preparing the fatted calf and welcoming Lacey into the fold, while I'd be stuttering and stammering, trying to figure out what to do with her."

Pensively, Mandy tapped the check against her palm as

she rounded the desk. "Sam's right, Merideth. It isn't your fault. But we've got to find her. She's a McCloud. There's no questioning that." She turned to look at her father's portrait and drew in a ragged breath. "For whatever reason, Lucas chose to deny her." She stared at the portrait a moment, then tore her gaze from the picture of the man who had made all his daughters' lives a living hell, and faced her sisters. "But we're not," she stated firmly. "She's family." She drew in a deep breath. "But first we've got to find her." Moving to stand before the window, she looked out at the darkness beyond, her brow furrowed. "Oh, my God!" she cried, her eyes suddenly widening.

"What is it?" Sam asked in alarm.

Mandy whirled. "She's at the barn," she cried, racing for the door. "Hurry! We've got to stop her before she leaves."

Lacey's horse danced nervously as she led him from the borrowed stall where Mandy's son had placed him earlier that afternoon. "It's okay, Buddy," she murmured softly, tightening her grip on the lead rope. "We're going home."

She led him through the barn's wide doors and out into the moonlit night. But once outside, the horse's uneasiness seemed to increase. He reared, nearly jerking Lacey off her feet. She quickly put slack in the line, and kept her voice low and soothing as she tried to calm him. "Too much strangeness, huh, Buddy? But it's okay now. We're heading home."

He snorted and tossed his head, prancing nervously around her as she slowly drew in the slack. When she was within reach, she stretched out a hand and rubbed his cheek, trying to calm him. Though he stilled, his head remained high, his ears pricked, his eyes wild and darting.

"There's nothing out here that's going to get you," she soothed. "Come on, Buddy," she urged and gave a gentle tug on the lead rope. "Let's load you in the trailer and we'll hit the road."

He followed skittishly, keeping tension on the line while he danced from side to side behind her. At the rear of the trailer, Lacey paused to swing open the double doors.

And heard Mandy call out to her.

"Lacey! Wait!"

"Come on, Buddy," she urged, panic surging through her. "In you go."

But the horse balked, sitting back on his haunches and pulling hard against the lead. Frustrated, she slapped the end of the rope across his rump. "Come on, Buddy," she cried, anxious to get away. "Get in there!"

At that moment, an armadillo darted from beneath the trailer and straight into the horse's path. The gelding reared, pawing at the air, then bolted forward, while the armadillo scuttled off into the darkness. Lacey jumped sideways, trying to get out of the horse's way, but the frightened animal slammed into her side, knocking her down. She hit the ground hard, grunting when her left hip took the brunt of the fall. With her face pressed into the dirt, she heard the dull thud of flesh hitting metal, then the horse's scream of pain. Her heart in her throat, she clawed her way to her feet. Dragging her sleeve across her face to clear the grit and tears from her eyes, she saw her horse standing ten feet away. He was trembling, blood oozing from a long gash on his shoulder.

Her breath burned painfully in her chest. "Buddy," she whispered brokenly. She limped slowly toward him,

stooping to pick up the end of the lead rope. She straightened, lifting her hand to fist her fingers in his mane, then
bent to examine the cut. "Oh, God, Buddy, what have
you done?" she sobbed, and buried her face against his
neck.

"Lacey."

She felt a hand go around her shoulders while another
gently pried the lead rope from her fingers. Sobbing, she
was pulled into Mandy's arms.

"He's h-hurt," she cried, trying to push away. "I've
got to take care of him."

"I know, honey," Mandy soothed, refusing to let her
go. "But Sam's a vet. She'll know what to do."

It would have been so easy to cling, to let someone else
take charge, to give in to the warmth and comfort she'd
been denied so long. But Lacey had been taking care of
herself and what was hers for too many years to relinquish
the control to someone else. Especially a McCloud. She
sniffed furiously and backed from Mandy's embrace, wiping a hand beneath her nose. She turned and saw Sam
kneeling beside Buddy, while Jaime stood at the horse's
head, holding the animal steady.

Gulping back the sob that threatened, she limped across
the short distance that separated them and dropped to her
knees beside Sam. "How bad is it?" she asked, unable
to keep the trembling from her voice.

"It's deep," Sam replied, frowning in concentration as
she smoothed a skilled hand down the horse's leg, check-
ing for other injuries. "But not as bad as I first thought."
She glanced up at her nephew. "Get my bag out of my
truck, Jaime. And I'll need some antibiotic. There should
be a vial in the refrigerator in the barn."

Her eyes wide with fear, Lacey watched Jaime jog

away into the night. "Can I haul him?" she asked anxiously, turning back to Sam.

"I wouldn't."

"But I have a rodeo next weekend."

Sam must have heard the desperation in her voice, because she spun slowly on the balls of her feet to face Lacey. "I'm afraid you're going to have to stay off of him longer than that."

Tears flooded Lacey's eyes, and Sam laid a comforting hand on her shoulder. "Why don't you stay here with us?" When Lacey opened her mouth to refuse, Sam squeezed. "Give him a week to heal. And a week for us to get to know you," she added softly.

Her hands still shook a little as Lacey made the turn at the Y in the road as Mandy had directed. On the seat beside her lay the key to the cabin, the concession she'd agreed to when Mandy had refused to allow her to drive into Austin to stay in a motel. Though all three of the McCloud sisters had offered her their homes, Lacey had refused their hospitality. The thought of the intimacy required in living for a week with any one of them was more than she felt she could handle. Her emotions were too raw, and much too close to the surface. Besides, she knew they'd already divvied up Jack and Alayna's six foster children between them and would have their hands full caring for them while the newlyweds were on their honeymoon. She didn't want to be a burden...but more, she didn't want to be in their debt.

She sighed wearily, thinking of Buddy bedded down in one of their stalls, of Sam tending his wound, and silently acknowledged that she was already in their debt.

Seeing the cabin ahead, she parked her truck alongside it, then grabbed her duffel bag from the seat behind her.

Climbing down, she groaned as pain shot into her hip, a result of the bruised muscle she'd gained in the fall. Limping gingerly, she headed for the porch and fumbled the key into the lock. She gave the door a push and stepped inside, feeling along the wall for the light switch. After flipping it on, she looked quickly around to get her bearings, then switched it off and headed for the far door and the bedroom beyond.

Once inside the room, she dropped her bag and reached for the light switch.

"Well, hello."

She jumped and whirled, a scream clawing its way up her throat. She nearly choked on it when she saw Travis lying in the bed, propped up on his elbows, grinning at her.

"What are *you* doing here?" she cried furiously.

Unconcerned, he sat up and plumped a pillow behind his head, then settled back against it. He folded his arms across his bare chest and smiled at her. "I was just about to ask you the same thing."

"Mandy gave me the key and told me I could stay here."

"My brother gave me a key and told me the same thing."

She stared at him, unable to prevent her gaze from slipping to the wall of muscled chest, the bulge of biceps on his folded arms, the sheet that draped his lower body from his navel down...and wondered if he was naked beneath it. Feeling the heat staining her neck, she jerked her gaze back to his. "B-but you can't stay here," she stammered. "*I* am."

He smiled and patted the mattress beside him. "There's room enough for two."

With a snort of disgust, Lacey snatched her duffel bag from the floor. "I'm not sharing a bed with you."

"Why not?" he returned, feigning innocence. "We're family."

"We are not!"

"Sure we are. My brother married your cousin, so that makes us family, too."

Infuriated by his twisted logic, she whirled for the bathroom. "I'm taking a shower, then I'm going to bed." At the door, she stopped and turned. "On the couch," she added tersely then slammed the door between them.

Travis heard the click of the lock, and tucked his hands behind his head, chuckling softly. Things were definitely looking up.

When he'd tried to talk to Jack again as his brother and his new wife were preparing to leave on their honeymoon, Jack had refused once again to listen to reason. Travis's threat that he was remaining at the ranch until he was sure that Jack wasn't making another mistake hadn't even fazed his brother. Jack had just tossed him the key to the cabin and told him that if he was staying to make himself at home, do a little fishing and maybe do a few repairs on the old barn.

Travis's smile broadened. Another week of his two-week vacation left to enjoy. A snug cabin, four lakes to fish and a beautiful woman to look at. Yeah, he thought smugly. Things were definitely looking up.

Lacey couldn't sleep. Her mind churned with the day's events and her chest ached with all the emotion bottled up inside.

A family, she kept telling herself over and over again. She had a family.

But she didn't want another family, she argued silently,

punching her pillow and bunching it beneath her cheek as she flopped over onto her side on the narrow couch. The one she'd left behind in Missouri had soured her for ever wanting another one.

The thought of her parents brought another swell of tears. All she'd ever wanted from them was their love, but they'd never been willing to give her even that. In retrospect, she could almost understand her stepfather's coolness toward her. After all, he wasn't her natural father, and he must have begrudged having to raise another man's child as his own.

Lucas. Her chest tightened painfully. He'd never even given her a chance. He'd simply turned his back on her and gone on with his life as if she had never existed.

And her mother...she choked on a sob and pressed her hand over her mouth to smother it. The one person who should have loved her, didn't. If anything, she resented Lacey. In her mother's eyes, Lacey had robbed her of her dreams, and every time she looked at her daughter she was reminded of that loss.

It didn't help that Lacey had succeeded where her mother had failed. A professional barrel racer, JoAnn Cline had been forced to give up her goal of winning a world championship when she'd discovered she was pregnant with Lacey. Lacey, though, without the encumbrance of a husband and children, had been free to pursue that dream, and was close, real close, to achieving her goal.

But not without Buddy.

Her lips trembled uncontrollably as her thoughts shifted to her horse and the injury he'd suffered. Without him she couldn't compete, and she'd lose her place in the standings and her chance for Las Vegas and a shot at the world title. But worse than the loss of the title was the thought of losing her best friend. And that was what Buddy was to her. They'd been a team for six years, traveling the circuit, sometimes even sharing a rented stall when Lacey lacked the funds for a motel room. In some ways, she felt closer to him than she did to her mother or her stepfather.

Squeezing her eyes shut, she tried to block out the disturbing thoughts.

But another, even more troubling image, slipped in to replace them.

Travis Cordell.

Even as she thought of him, the iron bed creaked in the other room, reminding her of his presence in the small cabin. She pulled the blanket to her chin, picturing him as he'd looked when she'd first discovered him in the cabin. Reared back against the headboard; that wall of muscled chest; wearing nothing but a rakish smile and a sheet draped low on his waist.

She remembered the feel of his arms around her from earlier that evening, when he'd pulled her onto his lap in the trailer, the magnetic pull of his sexy smile, the huskiness in his voice when he'd whispered his intention to make love with her on the trailer's narrow cot.

She flopped to her opposite side and bunched the pillow beneath her cheek. She didn't want to think about him. And she wouldn't, she told herself firmly.

My brother married your cousin, so that makes us family.

Cousins.

Half sisters.

Nieces and nephews.

Family.

She felt the tears rising again, and was helpless to keep them back as her thoughts churned full circle once again.

Travis awakened with a start, lifting his head from his pillow to listen. Slowly, he pushed himself to an elbow and stared at the closed door from behind which the sound came.

A shiver chased down his spine as the muffled sobs that had awakened him grew louder, more desperate.

What was going on? Was she hurt? Sick? Having a nightmare?

Not my problem, he told himself and dropped back down on the mattress, pulling the pillow over his head to block out the sound. She'd made it more than clear that she didn't want anything to do with him.

But the sobs continued, penetrating the thick down that covered his head and wearing on his nerves until he tossed the pillow aside with a growl and rolled to his feet. Muttering curses under his breath, he jerked on his jeans and stalked barefoot into the living room.

He stopped dead in his tracks when he saw her. Sitting on the sofa, limned by moonlight, her feet drawn up beneath her, her body bent almost double, her face buried in a pillow she held fisted across her lap. He couldn't remember ever seeing a more pitiful sight...or hearing a more heartbreaking sound.

"Lacey?" he called softly.

When she didn't respond, he crossed the room and hunkered down in front of her, bracing his hands on her knees. "Lacey. What's wrong?"

She jerked away from his touch, curling tighter into herself. "Leave me alone," she sobbed, her voice muffled by the pillow she kept pressed to her face.

Though there was nothing he'd like better, try as he might, Travis discovered he couldn't leave her. With a resigned sigh, he pushed himself to his feet, then sank down on the couch beside her, draping an arm along the back of the couch behind her. He stared at the top of her head a moment, unsure what to do, then sighed again. He dropped his hand on top of her head and scrubbed roughly. "Hey. Come on. Nothing's that bad."

"Go away," she wailed.

"Nope. Not until you stop your blubbering."

She lifted her head from the pillow to glare at him, her eyes red and swollen, tears streaming down her face. "I'll cry if I want to."

He cocked his head thoughtfully as if reminded of something. "Isn't there a song that goes something like that?" He hummed a few bars and then ducked, laughing, when she swung the pillow at him.

"Why can't you just leave me alone?" she cried furiously.

He sobered quickly and cleared his throat. "Sorry. I was just trying to make you laugh."

"Well, I'm not laughing." She jerked the pillow back to her lap, wadding it into a ball, and stubbornly turned her face away from him.

"You're not crying, either," he pointed out gently.

And she didn't want to cry any more. Especially not in front of him. But the tears were there, pushing at her throat. She shook back her hair and inhaled deeply, valiantly fighting them back.

"I guess you've had a pretty tough day, huh?" he said, watching her carefully.

She sniffed and dashed a finger beneath her nose. "I've had better."

"The McClouds seem nice enough."

Remembering Merideth and her caustic remarks, she replied bitterly, "Most of them."

"So what's the problem?"

"You wouldn't understand."

"Try me."

She pressed her lips together as much in frustration as to hold back the tears. "I said I don't want to talk about it."

"Well, I do."

She whirled to glare at him. "Why don't you just go back to bed?"

"I will, if you'll come with me."

She snorted her opinion of his suggestion and whipped around to face the wall again.

He scooted closer. "Come on, Lacey. Why don't you tell me what's bothering you? Sometimes talking helps."

He watched her chest swell and her chin quiver as she fought back the tears. But in spite of her efforts, a tear slipped over her lower lashes and slid down her cheek. Another quickly followed.

"Aw, Lace," he said gruffly, and wrapped his arm around her shoulders, hugging her hard against his side. "Don't start crying again."

She struggled, obviously not wanting his comfort, but he tightened his hold on her, refusing to let her go. He felt a shudder move through her and when she tried to bury her face in the pillow again, he tugged it from her hands and tossed it aside. He forced her face against his shoulder, and it was as if he'd pulled the plug on a dam. He could feel the sobs that ripped through her body, the hot tears that scalded his arm and chest...and did what he felt any man would do in his place.

Prayed the well would soon run dry.

But in spite of his prayers, the sobs continued both in intensity and volume, until they echoed in his head and reverberated through his body.

"Lacey," he said in concern, leaning to smooth her hair from her face. "You've got to stop or you're going to make yourself sick."

But she only cried that much harder.

"Is there something I can get you? Water? Aspirin?" When she didn't respond, he dipped his chin and turned her face up toward his. "Isn't there anything I can do?"

The eyes that met his were flooded with tears. "H-he didn't w-want me."

"Lucas?"

She hiccuped a sob and nodded, then buried her face in her hands, her shoulders heaving violently.

He wrapped his arm tighter around her. "His mistake," he said gruffly. "The guy must have been an ass."

"M-my parents d-didn't want me, e-either."

"That's not true," he argued gently. He smoothed a hand over her hair, trying to comfort her. "All parents love their kids. There's an unwritten law somewhere that says they have to, no matter what."

"M-mine d-don't," she sobbed hysterically.

"Aw, Lacey," he said, his voice growing husky. He drew her against his side and squeezed. "Nobody's worth this many tears."

If she heard him, she didn't respond. And she sure as heck didn't quit crying. Heaving a frustrated sigh, Travis tipped her chin up. "Come on, now. Surely there must be something that I can do to make you feel better?"

The eyes that looked up at him were flooded with tears. "H-hold m-me."

He shook his head to clear his ears, sure that he'd misunderstood her. "Hold you?" he repeated.

Her breath hitched as she bobbed her head.

"Okay," he said hesitantly and wrapped his other arm loosely around her, drawing her within his embrace. When he did, she threw her arms around his neck on a strangled sob, and pressed her body against his. His eyes widened in surprise at the strength, the desperation with which she clung to him. Moments ago she'd been shoving him away, demanding that he leave, and now she was clinging to him as if she was drowning and he was the only lifeboat around.

Even as he thought this, he became aware of other things. How small and fragile she felt in his arms, how defenseless, unlike the image she'd projected earlier. Tough. Independent. That I-don't-need-anybody-and-I'm-getting-along-just-fine-on-my-own attitude that she wore so well.

In spite of his reluctance to offer her comfort, he found himself drawing her more closely within his embrace. He could feel the heat of her body pressed against his, the almost manic beat of her heart against his chest. Her tears scalded his neck, and ran down his chest.

She needed him.

And Travis never allowed anyone to get close enough to need him for anything.

He swallowed back the emotion that rose in his throat. He knew what it was like to yearn for human comfort, to need so badly it hurt, and have no one to turn to with whom to share the pain. Though his was a self-inflicted banishment, one he'd orchestrated after Jack's first marriage, a secret that ate like a cancer at his soul, he figured that his and Lacey's situations weren't all that different. Neither one of them had family they could turn to.

Over the years, he'd taught himself to do without the love and support of his family, and to take what warmth and comfort he could from whatever physical relationships he became involved in. But he did so without committing himself to anything or anyone in return. As a result, he'd developed a style that other men envied. He could sweet-talk his way into a woman's bed and out of it just as quickly, without leaving any hard feelings behind when he left. Sweet talkin', hard lovin' man. That's the name he'd earned. And that's the image he wanted to keep.

But when he slipped his hand to Lacey's hip to shift her onto his lap, he wasn't thinking about sex, or how he might sweet-talk this woman into his bed. He was just doing as she'd asked. Holding her. Giving her the comfort she seemed to need so desperately.

Yet when he eased her across his lap, and his hand slid from her hip to her thigh, his palm meeting bare skin…his thoughts shifted away from comfort and came danger-ously close to lust. Her skin was so soft, he thought in wonder, so warm to the touch. He could imagine it heating even more when aroused.

Her breath hitched once, and she buried her face in the curve of his neck, locking her arms more tightly around him. He could feel the fullness of her breasts flattened against his chest, the almost painful dig of her pelvic bone against his groin…yet another reminder of the intimacy of their position. It would be so easy to just ease her down onto the couch and stretch out beside her. To kiss her and touch her until she forgot all about her problems. To fill his hands with her ripe, full breasts, suckle them until she was begging him to make love to her.

Don't even think it, Cordell, he warned himself. This isn't the time or the place.

She shifted and he sucked in a raw breath when her hip grazed his manhood. He wanted to hold her there, feel the warmth of her femininity nestled around him…but he couldn't. His conscience wouldn't let him.

On a low, frustrated groan, he let his head fall back against the couch and squeezed his eyes shut. Of all the times to decide to become a Boy Scout, Cordell, he re-flected miserably, you picked a hell of a good one.

With a resigned sigh, he continued to hold her, unconsciously stroking her thigh, his palm moving up and down her bare leg in slow, soothing strokes. When his knuckles hit the edge of the T-shirt she wore, he scrupulously reversed the movement, smoothing his palm down to her bent knee again, trying to keep his thoughts chaste.

He rubbed his cheek against her hair. "Don't cry, Lace," he whispered at her ear. "Come on, baby. Don't cry anymore."

But it seemed as if she couldn't stop.

And Travis couldn't let her go. He continued to hold her until his arms ached, his rear end grew numb and his voice was hoarse from whispering unintelligible words of comfort. He held her until, with a last shuddery sigh, she burrowed deeper against his chest, laid a hand over his heart, and grew quiet.

Fearing that any movement from him would make her start crying again, he continued to stroke her leg. With each slow movement upward, her T-shirt rose a little higher on her thigh, until his fingertips brushed the elastic of her panties.

Relaxed now, his mind dulled by exhaustion, he slipped a finger beneath the thin band and slowly traced its edge. Back and forth. Back and forth. The calluses on his palm chafing against her tender skin. From the inside of her thigh to the swell of her buttocks. Back and forth. Back and forth in a mindless journey to nowhere.

He felt a shudder pass through her, felt her fingers curl into a fist against his chest. Slowly she pressed that fist against him and lifted her head until their gazes met. The eyes that met his were red-rimmed but dry.

And filled with an unmistakable heat.

His gaze on hers, he slipped his finger guiltily from beneath the elastic. He watched her throat move as she gulped a breath. Uncertainly, he brushed her hair back, then drew his palms to her cheeks to frame her face. Teardrops glistened on the tips of her lower lashes and the end of her nose was red from crying.

Never had a woman looked so beautiful to him, nor so desirable.

"Lacey," he murmured as he smoothed his thumbs beneath her lashes, stealing the last traces of her tears. She looked up at him, her eyes filled with an endearing blend of wonder and need. Her lips were moist and full and only a breath away.

Unable to resist, he lowered his mouth to hers. He tasted the salt from her tears and something sweeter. Something warm and needy that drew him deeper into the kiss.

Wrapping his arms more tightly around her, he drew the kiss out, tasting and exploring. Surprised that she didn't shove him away, demand that he get his hands off her, he eased back to look at her. He saw himself so clearly in the depths of her green eyes. A misfit. An outsider. Someone with a need so strong for human warmth that it was almost a pain, but one who didn't dare ever let down his guard long enough to accept that warmth when it was offered.

They were so much alike.

Yet so different.

A fissure opened in his heart, and the strangest, most powerful feeling swelled in his chest and spread through his body. He wanted to hold her, make love to her, give her the warmth and comfort she so desperately wanted. He wanted to make up for all the pain she'd suffered in her life.

"Lacey," he whispered. But then their lips were pressed tightly again.

Only this time it was she who made the move, and words became impossible, unnecessary.

Three

Travis didn't try to stop her. He couldn't. Didn't want to. He wanted only to feel. And the woman pressing herself against him felt damn good and tasted even better. Without breaking the kiss, he shifted, drawing her legs around him until she straddled his lap, their bodies flush, her breasts flattened against his chest.

Groaning his pleasure at the feel of her soft seductive curves pressing against him, he smoothed his hands up the backs of her thighs and cupped her bottom, molding her tighter against him. But when her feminine mound met the column of his quickly hardening arousal, a shudder moved through her and he experienced a moment's panic.

An aftershock from all the emotion she'd spent? he wondered uneasily. A sign that she was revolted by his touch? Or was it her body's way of telling him that she was enjoying their closeness as much as he?

Hoping it was the latter, he locked his arms around her
and pushed himself to his feet, guiding her legs around
his waist. He stood for a moment with his mouth still
locked over hers, waiting, giving her a chance to object.
When she didn't offer any protests, he headed for the
bedroom. At the side of the old iron bed, he buried a knee
in the mattress, the ancient springs creaking beneath their
joined weight as he lowered her and followed her down.

When she was lying beneath him, then, and only then,
did he dare break the kiss. Bracing his hands on either
side of her head, he withdrew far enough to look down
at her face. Moonlight danced over cheeks flushed with
passion and painted shadows beneath thick, still-damp
lashes. Her lips, slightly parted, were moist and swollen
from his kisses, and her chest rose and fell with each
labored breath she drew.

Where was the woman who had fought with him, argued with him, shunned his earlier advances? And who
was this devastatingly beautiful woman, eyes wide with
uncertainty, who responded to his every touch? Certain
that he was dreaming, he lifted a hand and brushed a
wayward strand of hair from her cheek…just to be sure
that she was real, that she wasn't part of some dream he'd
wake from. When his knuckles grazed her skin, their
gazes met and locked. Green eyes burned into brown.

And he knew this was no dream. And he knew, too,
that he had to have her.

"Lacey, I want to make—"

She pressed two fingertips against his lips, silencing
him, then lifted her head, replacing the fingers with her
lips, and gave him the answer to the question she wouldn't
let him voice.

She kissed him until his breath burned in his lungs and
his heart beat like something wild in his chest. Gasping,

he broke away from her and pushed to his knees, rocking back on his heels to look down at her, wanting to do more than just taste, wanting desperately to put his hands on her. Placing a fingertip in the hollow of her throat, he drew his finger down to the neckline of her T-shirt, bunching the fabric down into the valley between her breasts. He stared a moment at the creamy skin he'd bared, then, unable to resist, leaned over, and pressed a kiss into the shadowed recess.

He heard her sharp inhalation of breath as his tongue stroked her flesh, felt against his lips the tremble of the shuddery sigh that followed. He shifted to nip at a breast through the T-shirt's thin fabric, then sank back on his heels again. He cupped his hands over the swollen mounds, molding their shape. "You are one beautiful woman," he murmured appreciatively.

He rubbed his thumbs over her nipples, watching them harden, then smoothed his hands up and over her breasts, down her stomach, dipping into the curve of her waist and out again until his palms lay splayed over her abdomen.

Soft. Lean. Curvy. Perfect, he decided with a satisfied sigh.

He slipped a finger beneath the elastic of her panties and slowly traced the band. He heard her breath quicken, felt the quiver of reaction in her thigh. Glancing up, he watched the heat glaze her eyes. Holding her gaze, he hooked his finger over the top band and slowly pulled the scrap of silk down, baring her abdomen inch by slow inch.

"Mmm," he moaned in anticipation and dipped his face over her stomach to lap at the delectable skin above her femininity. His tongue followed the silk's slow journey as he pulled her panties over her hips until his lips were pressed on the inside of her thigh. He nibbled at the tender flesh, then raised his head and looked up at her, a slow smile building. "And sweet, too."

Her eyes filled with tears again. "Hey," he scolded gently. "No more crying." Concerned that he'd upset her again, he stretched out beside her and laid a palm against her cheek, turning her face to his. "Was it something I said? Something I did?"

She shook her head and closed her hand over his, holding it against her cheek. "No," she said, trying valiantly to hold back the tears. "It's just that—" She gulped and tried again. "It's just that you're being so kind."

Chuckling, he pulled her into his arms and hugged her to him. "Me? Kind? Baby, you've obviously forgotten about that little scuffle I had with my brother this afternoon."

She tipped her face up to his and, lifting a hand, touched a fingertip to the bandage she'd placed on his temple earlier that day. "You fought with him because you cared."

He chuckled again, shaking his head. "Don't kid yourself, Lace. My heart's as black as cast iron and twice as hard."

Before she could argue the point with him, he closed his mouth over hers. "I want to make love with you," he murmured against her lips. "I want to make you forget all your troubles for a while." He closed a hand over her breast and rubbed his palm across her nipple, feeling it bud against the thin fabric that covered it, before shifting his gaze to hers again. "We're gonna be good together," he said and stretched to nip at her lower lip. "I can promise you that."

Lacey didn't doubt that he was a good lover. Even as he made the promise, the most delicious sensations spread from her breasts all the way to her toes, making them curl. And, for the moment, she needed the escape he offered, to have her mind stripped free of all the emotion that churned there.

She needed to forget.

Desperate for the mindless release he promised, she wrapped her arms around his neck and drew his face to hers. She drank deeply, absorbing the heat, the passion, until desire burned through her and crowded out all other thoughts but those of him.

He groaned, shifting over her. "Damn, you taste good," he growled and plunged his tongue deeply into her mouth as if he intended to devour her. He probed the velvety recesses of her mouth, mating his tongue with hers, then rolled to his back, bringing her with him. He matched her length to his, shifting her hips slightly until his arousal nestled in the curve of her pelvic bone. All the while, he plundered her mouth with his tongue and roamed her back with his hands.

"Lacey," he groaned, frustrated by the last thin layer of fabric that separated them. "I want to feel you, see you."

She tore her mouth from his, and pushed back to meet his gaze. He saw the uncertainty there, as well as the need. Then she slowly braced her hands against his chest and pushed herself up to a sitting position, straddling him. Gathering the hem of her T-shirt, she pulled it over her head and tossed it aside. Her breasts swelled on a deeply drawn breath, then rose higher, teasing him with their dark pink centers as she lifted her arms to flip her auburn hair back over her shoulders. Her gaze lowered to his chest, and her eyes darkened and smoldered.

With a tenderness he knew he didn't deserve, she placed her hands high on his chest and smoothed them down in an erotic sweeping motion to his navel then back again until her palms came to a rest in the center of his rib cage.

"I can feel your heart beating," she whispered, seemingly awed by the discovery. Before he could deny that he had one, she lowered her face to press her lips to the spot.

He squeezed his eyes shut and gritted his teeth, emotion swelling in his chest. He groaned as her lips grazed his sensitized skin. Unable to bear the sweetness, the tenderness of her touch, he reached for her and drew her back to him. He covered her mouth with his as he rolled, placing her beneath him again. Kicking free of his jeans, he wedged a knee between hers, spreading them and making a nest for himself.

"Do I need protection?" he asked as he sought her mouth again.

"No. I—" She gasped when his hardness pressed against her feminine opening, then sighed, filling her hands with his hair and drawing his face closer to hers.

Pleasure rose, blinding Lacey to everything but the overpowering need to have him inside her. "Take me," she begged him, the plea a raw, desperate whisper. "Please. Take me."

He set his jaw. "My pleasure," he growled and thrust deeply inside her. She arched, rising to meet him, and dug her fingers into his back in an effort to draw him deeper still. Pressing her head back against the pillows, she cried out his name...then slowly melted beneath him, her chest heaving with each panted breath. He held his position for a full beat, watching her lids grow heavy, the flush of pleasure stain her cheeks. Then he began to move, slowly, drawing her with him. With each slow stroke, her breath grew shorter, more ragged and her hands more desperate as they moved over his back and buttocks, forcing him closer, deeper.

Knowing she was hovering dangerously close to the oblivion he'd promised her, he dragged his lips down her chin, over her jaw, and closed them over her breast. Drawing her deeply into his mouth, he tucked a hand beneath her hips, lifted, and plunged one last time.

She arched high, her blunt nails digging into his back...then she came apart in his hands, sobbing out his name again and again. Nearly blinded by the velvet hammer-like blows of her climax pulsing around him, he threw back his head and, with a growl, emptied his seed into her. Shuddering, he sank, weakened and spent, against her and buried his face in the curve of her neck.

He could feel the thunder of their joined hearts, the warmth of her breath at his ear, taste the sweetness of her skin beneath his lips, the tenderness in the palm that rested over his heart.

And wondered who had comforted who.

Travis awakened slowly, feeling more relaxed and rested than he had in months. Knowing the reason why, he stretched lazily, a satisfied smile building on his face, then rolled to his side and reached for Lacey.

But his hand found only tangled covers. Opening his eyes fully, he lifted his head. Sunshine spilled through the window opposite him, spotlighting the empty bed beside him.

He pushed himself to an elbow and glanced around. "Lacey?" When she didn't answer, he rolled to his feet and padded naked into the living room. "Lacey?" he called again. Crossing to the window, he shoved back the drapes and peered outside.

The spot beneath the tree where she'd parked her truck the night before was as empty as his bed.

The disappointment that surged through him both surprised and angered him. He wasn't used to a woman leaving him without so much as a goodbye. Usually, he was the one sneaking off to avoid the awkwardness of the morning after, or the claw of a woman's clinging hands.

Scowling, he dropped the drape and headed for the bathroom.

Lacey kept the water hose aimed at the wound on her horse's shoulder as she slowly massaged his foreleg with her free hand. "How's that feel, Buddy?" she asked, looking up at him. "Better?"

In answer, the animal snorted, then blew, bumping his nose against the top of her head. She chuckled, and continued with her massage. "Yeah, well, my turn's next," she warned him. "My hip's pretty stiff from that fall you made me take last night."

"You should have told me you hurt your hip. I give a pretty good massage, even if I do say so myself."

Startled, Lacey spun on the balls of her feet at the sound of Travis's voice, then frowned when she saw him standing behind her, watching her, his arms folded accusingly across his chest. His hair was still wet from his shower, and he'd shaved away the dark stubble of beard. Dressed in a blue chambray shirt and faded jeans, he should have looked less threatening than he had when he'd tried to stop the wedding. But he didn't. If anything, he looked more dangerous. More desirable.

Feeling the heat creep up her neck, she turned her back to him and aimed the water hose at Buddy's wound again. "It's no big deal. Just a bruise."

Hoping he'd get the message and leave her alone, she

was disappointed when he hunkered down beside her, his knee brushing against hers. "What happened?" he asked, gesturing toward the horse's wound.

"He spooked last night when I was trying to load him in the trailer and slammed his shoulder against the door."

"Bad?"

"Bad enough," she said with regret as she smoothed a hand close to the long gash. Sighing wearily, she pushed to her feet, and twisted the nozzle, shutting off the water's flow.

Travis stood, too. "Why didn't you wake me up this morning when you left?"

She lifted a shoulder, but refused to look at him as she crossed to turn off the faucet. "Figured you needed the sleep."

He took the hose from her and wound it around the iron rim where it was stored, leaving her with nothing to do but watch. When he finished the task, he turned and took her by the elbows, catching her unawares, and drew her to him. Her gaze snapped to his, her eyes wide with surprise.

"Not as badly as I needed this," he told her, his voice bedroom soft as he lowered his face over hers.

When Lacey opened her mouth to insist that he let her go, he plunged his tongue between her parted lips, making her heart shoot to her throat, her blood pound in her ears. Feeling her resistance weakening, she braced her hands against his chest, and eased from his embrace.

"Look," she said, gulping a breath. "Last night was...well, it was a mistake, okay?" She'd decided that when she'd first awakened, still wrapped snugly in his arms. And it was because she had discovered she liked the feel of his arms around her, the warmth of his body curled protectively around hers, that she had slipped from the bed without waking him. She'd learned years ago not to allow herself to need, to want. She always ended up disappointed when she did.

She took another step back from temptation. "I appreciate you—well, taking care of me, but I'm okay now. See?" she said, lifting her arms out to her sides, and forcing a smile. "No more hysterics."

She watched his eyes darken, his jaw tense, and plunged on before he had a chance to argue the point with her. "I figure we can share the cabin without any problem. You can have the bed. I'll take the couch. It's only for a couple of days, right?" She forced a laugh. "We're adults. I'm sure we can manage to stay out of each other's hair for that short a period of time."

Travis's insides quivered with fury as he listened to her rattle on. A mistake? Is that what she had called one of the most memorable nights of his life? And she expected him to act as if nothing had happened? To share the cabin with her and not touch her again?

He narrowed his eyes, looking at her more closely, and noted the way she kept lacing and unlacing her fingers, the false bravado in her smile.

And wondered who she was trying to convince. Him or herself?

Well, two can play this game, he told himself. And he had more than enough time to prove to her just how wrong she was. Pleased by this knowledge, he shot her a wink. "Piece of cake," he agreed easily. "A couple of days, and then we go our separate ways." Touching a finger to his forehead, he turned and strolled away, whistling merrily.

Lacey slid the latch into place, then laid her arms along the top of the stall door and dropped her chin on her hands as she watched Buddy head for the trough and the feed she'd placed there for him.

Three, maybe four days, she thought miserably. How in the heck was she supposed to share a cabin with Travis for that length of time without crawling into his bed again?

"How's he doing?"

She jumped at the sound of Mandy's voice, then forced herself to relax when her half sister moved to stand beside her. "Okay, I guess. I did the water therapy as Sam suggested and walked him for a while. His leg doesn't seem as stiff as it did earlier this morning."

"Good." Mandy folded her arms along the stall gate, mirroring Lacey's stance, and watched the horse tug a mouthful of hay from the rack. "Doesn't seem to have affected his appetite any," she said, biting back a smile.

"Buddy?" Lacey sputtered a laugh. "It would take more than a cut on the shoulder to slow him down. He's made of pretty tough stuff."

Mandy angled her head to peer at Lacey. "And so are you." Lacey's brows shot up and Mandy laughed, reaching over to give her arm a pat. "That was meant as a compliment."

"Oh, well..." Lacey stammered in embarrassment.

Mandy laughed again and turned her back to the gate, folding her arms beneath her breasts. "Travis stopped by the house earlier."

Lacey felt the heat crawl up her neck, but kept her gaze on her horse. "He did?"

"Uh-huh. He told me that he was staying in the cabin, too, that Jack had given him a key. Is that a problem for you?"

The heat made it to Lacey's cheeks and burned there. Though tempted to take advantage of Mandy's earlier offer of hospitality, she quickly decided that remaining in the cabin with Travis would be easier—the lesser of two evils. "No," she said. "No problem. The cabin's big enough for two without us getting in each other's hair." She pushed away from the stall gate and, stuffing her hands deep into her pockets, chipped the toe of her boot against the hard-packed dirt, avoiding Mandy's gaze.

Mandy watched her and wondered if Lacey realized how much she looked like Sam at that moment. When uncomfortable or when trying to hide her feelings, Sam had a habit of stuffing her hands in her pockets and hunching her shoulders in much the same way as Lacey was doing now. She wondered, too, what feelings Lacey might be trying to hide.

Could there be something developing between her and Travis? They'd known each other for less than twenty-four hours, yet she couldn't think of another explanation for the sudden spots of color on Lacey's cheeks or her unease at the mention of Travis's name. Travis and Lacey. Mandy thought about that a moment, then quickly decided that the two might be perfect for each other.

Deciding to help things along, she slipped her arm through Lacey's and guided her out of the barn. "Well, if it becomes a problem, let me know, and we'll make room for you in the house."

"Sure thing."

Mandy gave Lacey's arm a squeeze and glanced over at her. "Would you mind doing me a favor?"

Relieved to have the opportunity to tip the scales a little in her favor after all that the McClouds had done for Buddy, Lacey said, "Sure. What do you need me to do?"

At the back door, Mandy stopped and turned to Lacey, her expression turning hesitant. "Well, I hate to impose, but I'm a bit swamped at the moment, what with all the kids here and the wranglers due in for lunch at any moment. I was wondering if you'd mind taking Travis a bite to eat? He said that he was going to work on the roof of Jack and Alayna's barn, and I really don't have the time to drive over there to take him his lunch, not with what all else I've got to do.''

Lacey felt her stomach knot in dread at the thought of having to face Travis again. But how could she refuse when Mandy had been so kind to her? She inhaled deeply, then exhaled, letting the breath out slowly. ''Sure,'' she said, forcing a note of enthusiasm into her voice. ''No problem.''

Lacey heard him before she saw him. The metallic ping of a hammer hitting tin, his whistled accompaniment to the country music blaring from the jam box that sat on a sawhorse beside the ladder propped against the side of the barn. Shading her eyes, she looked up and found him hunkered down on the barn's roof, his back to her, hammering a new sheet of tin into place. Sweat ran in rivulets down his back and moistened the waist of his jeans. Muscles bunched and corded on his back and arm with each rhythmic swing of the hammer.

Her gaze moved from his broad shoulders to trail along his spine to the strip of lighter skin showing just above the waist of his jeans.

Her mouth suddenly dry, she swallowed hard. ''There ought to be a law,'' she muttered under her breath, then shouted, ''Hey, Travis! I brought you some lunch.''

When he didn't respond, she huffed a breath and marched over to the jam box and switched it off. She stepped back and looked up, waiting. Within seconds his head appeared over the edge of the barn's roof, his eyes narrowed in aggravation.

Frowning, she held up the bag. "I brought you something to eat."

His grin was slow and devastating as it spread across his face. "I'll be right there."

He turned his back to her, swung a leg over the ladder, then planted a boot on its top rung and started down. She told herself she wasn't going to stand there and watch him like some over-sexed teenager, but quickly discovered she couldn't tear her eyes away. With each step downward, the muscles in his butt and thighs corded, holding her in place. By the time he reached the ground, her lungs felt like a furnace, overheated and ready to blow.

He turned, wiping his hands across the seat of his jeans, his smile broadening as he crossed to her. "What did you bring me? I'm starving."

Her breath came out in a rush of air. "Uh—fried chicken, I think, and s-some of that potato salad they served last night at the reception."

He hooked an arm around her neck and headed her toward the side of the barn and the shade there. "Fried chicken. Mmm-mmm. My favorite." He stretched an arm across her front to take the bag and his arm chafed against her breasts. Millions of tiny electrical shocks ripped through Lacey's system and her fingers slipped numbly from the bag.

Travis caught the sack and slipped his arm from around her to open it. Sticking his nose inside, he inhaled deeply. He closed his eyes on a lusty sigh and let his head loll back. "I think I'm in love," he said, then opened his eyes and grinned at her.

He dropped down on the ground and pulled out a chicken leg. Settling his back against the barn wall, he patted the ground beside him and looked up at her. "Have a seat," he invited and took a bite.

Lacey stared at him, wondering how on earth a man could make eating a chicken leg look so erotic. "N-no." She took a step back. "I better go."

Travis caught the hem of her jeans, stopping her. "What's the hurry?" he asked, teasing her with another grin. "Afraid you won't be able to keep your hands off me?"

With a huff of disgust, Lacey plopped down beside him. "Your ego's showing again," she muttered darkly and snatched the sack from his lap. She pulled out a piece of chicken and clamped her teeth viciously into the succulent meat, imagining that it was *him* she was taking a bite of.

Travis chuckled and settled his back more comfortably against the wall, purposefully letting his shoulder bump against hers. She jumped at the contact, frowned, then shifted away.

He tossed back his head and laughed. "Oh, this is going to be fun," he said, still chuckling as he dipped his hand into the sack again.

Scowling, Lacey turned to look at him. "What is?"

He glanced over and smiled. "Watching you try to resist me."

Whistling through his teeth, Travis stepped from the shadows of the woods and strolled toward the cabin. He had a string of trout draped over his shoulder, and a firm grip on his favorite rod and reel. He didn't figure a man could get much closer to heaven than this. Four lakes to fish. A pretty woman to seduce. And plenty of time on his hands to pursue both pleasures.

When he reached the cabin, he propped his fishing gear

by the front door before stepping inside. In the kitchen, he dumped the fish into the sink, then rummaged through drawers, looking for a knife. Finding one, he pulled it out and pressed the pad of his thumb against the blade, testing its sharpness.

The screen door squeaked open behind him and he glanced over his shoulder just as Lacey stumbled through the doorway, loaded down with bulging shopping bags.

"Whatcha got there?" he asked, nodding toward the bags.

She swung them up onto the counter, frowning. "Groceries."

He bit back a grin, knowing by her frown that she was still peeved with him for teasing her earlier about her not being able to resist him. He turned a hip against the counter and watched as she yanked canned goods from the sack. "I thought we were supposed to take our meals at the house with Mandy's family?"

"I don't like crowds." She stretched to stash her purchases in the cupboard overhead.

He watched her drop back down to her heels and tug her shirt into place...and couldn't resist teasing her a little more. He stepped quickly behind her, wrapped his arms around her waist and nuzzled his nose in the crook of her neck. "Yeah. Dinner for two does sound a lot more romantic."

Her elbow connected soundly with his stomach, and he bent double, choking on a laugh.

"Jerk," she muttered and shoved past him. Snatching a gallon of milk from a sack, she rammed it against his chest. "Make yourself useful."

Still chuckling, Travis took the jug, opened the refrigerator and slid it inside. "What all did you buy?" he asked, dipping his head over one of the sacks.

"Food. And if you think I'm doing all the cooking, you've—" She stopped mid-sentence and clamped a hand over her mouth and nose. "What is that awful odor?" she cried.

"Dinner." He nodded toward the sink and she leaned over, her hand still clamped tightly over her nose and mouth. "What's the matter?" he asked, trying not to laugh as he watched her pale. "Don't you like fish?"

She turned away with a shudder. "Yeah. Battered and fried," she said dryly.

Travis picked up the knife again. "I could do that," he said agreeably, then added, "But I was thinking more along the lines of grilling them." He unhooked a trout from the string, and laid it out over the cutting board. "A little butter and some roasted garlic. A touch of lemon. Maybe some dill." He cocked his head to look at her. "Did you happen to buy any fresh herbs while you were in town?"

She stared at him a full two seconds. "Fresh herbs?" she repeated slowly. "What are you? Some kind of gourmet chef?"

He chuckled and angled the knife at the trout's gills, preparing to clean the fish. "You might think so once you taste my cooking."

The mouthwatering odors drifting beneath the bathroom door were slowly driving Lacey mad. Trying to ignore them, she wound her wet hair on top of her head and stuck a wooden pick in the knot to hold it in place.

Real men don't cook.

She snorted a laugh as she dropped her arms to her sides, remembering her stepfather's favorite excuse to avoid sharing cooking duties with Lacey and her mother.

And they'd fallen for his lame excuse every time—hook, line and sinker.

Well, that rationalization certainly didn't wash any more, she thought wryly as she pushed an arm through the sleeve of an oversized shirt. She'd never met a manlier man than Travis Cordell, and if the scents coming from the kitchen were any indication, he could *definitely* cook.

Snorting a laugh, she drew the shirt's plackets together, then froze, her gaze riveted on her reflection in the mirror. Leaning closer to the glass, she touched a fingertip to the tiny bruise above her left breast…and knew immediately how she'd come by the mark. A love bite. A passion mark. Whatever term it was currently called, Travis had given it to her.

She drew in a deep breath, covering the mark with her hand. But she couldn't stop the wave of desire that rose along with the memory of his clever mouth suckling and nipping at her bare flesh. It clamped like a fist low in her abdomen and twisted, robbing her of her ability to breathe. Dropping her hands to the edge of the sink, she curled her fingers against the chipped porcelain and hauled in a steadying breath. She wouldn't let him get to her, she told herself. She couldn't.

"Hey, Lace!"

She jerked to attention at the sound of Travis's voice and snatched the plackets of her shirt across her breasts. "What?" she called and began to frantically fasten buttons.

"Dinner's ready."

"I'll be right there." She quickly finished buttoning her shirt and stepped back to check her reflection in the mirror. When she saw the amount of bare skin still showing at her neck, she frowned and fastened the top button. Taking another step back, she smoothed her hands down her hips and inhaled deeply before opening the bathroom door and peeking outside.

The bedroom was dark and there was no sign of Travis anywhere near. She tiptoed to the bedroom door and peered into the living room beyond, wondering where he'd gone. She discovered him standing by a small table set for two, one hand cupped around the top of a tall tapered candle while with the other he touched the flame of a match to the candle's wick. As it caught, candlelight danced on the rough-hewn walls and bounced off the ceiling, quickly filling the darkened room with a soft romantic glow.

He glanced up and saw her standing frozen in the doorway. He lifted the match to his lips and blew it out, then smiled.

"Hungry?"

Stunned, she could only stare. He had to be the most handsome, most virile man on the planet. Standing there barefoot, dressed in jeans and with the cuffs of his chambray shirt rolled to his elbows, his hair brushing the collar of his shirt and falling boyishly over his forehead, that woman-killing smile of his turned her insides to putty.

Feeling the heat rising to her cheeks, she forced her gaze away from him and to the table. Plates, silverware, napkins. A bottle of wine, open and waiting. He'd even filled an old jar with wild flowers and set it in the center of the table.

When she didn't respond, he pulled out a chair and gestured in invitation. "The trout's best if eaten while it's still warm," he teased.

Knowing very well why he'd gone to all the trouble, Lacey tore her gaze from the table and narrowed it on him. "I won't let you seduce me."

Four

Chuckling, Travis crossed to Lacey and took her by the hand. "Who said anything about seducing you?"

"You didn't have to." She looked pointedly at the table. "If that isn't a scene set for seduction, I'll eat my hat."

"No need to do that," he said and gave her hand a tug. "I've grilled trout that'll taste a whole lot better."

Reluctantly, she allowed him to lead her to the table, then tossed a frown over her shoulder when he insisted on holding her chair for her as she sat down.

After she was seated, he slid onto the chair opposite hers and picked up the bottle of wine. "I raided Jack's liquor cabinet while you were in the shower." He angled the bottle to read the label. "I hope you like chardonnay. Personally, I think a nice chablis would be better with the trout, but this was all I could find."

Determined to remain unimpressed, she shook out her

napkin and spread it across her lap. "Chablis?" she said, arching a brow. "I'd think your taste would run closer to beer."

Making a tsking sound with his tongue, he tipped the bottle over her glass and poured. "Never judge a book by its cover." He filled his own glass, then lifted it, smiling at her over its rim. "To us."

She picked up her glass and frowned. "There is no us."

He leaned across the table and clicked his glass against hers. "Sure there is. There's you," he said, tipping his glass toward her. "And then there's me," he said and touched the bowl of his glass to his chest. "You plus me equals us." Smiling, he reared back in his chair and lifted the glass to his lips, teasing her with a smile over its rim.

She snorted and took a sip of her wine, then quickly set it down and picked up her fork, determined not to fall prey to his charm. "I won't let you seduce me," she told him again.

"So you said." With a sigh, he set aside his glass. "Well, if you're not going to let me seduce you, then I guess we'll just have to eat."

Sure that she'd choke on anything that she tried to swallow, Lacey levered a small piece of the grilled trout from her plate and into her mouth. Her eyes went round. "Oh, my gosh!" she exclaimed and immediately scooped up another forkful. "This is wonderful," she said around a mouthful of the succulent fish. She closed her eyes, letting the flavors dance over her taste buds, then swallowed and sighed appreciatively.

"Like it?"

She flipped open her eyes to stare at him in dismay. "Like it! It's...it's..."

"Better than sex?"

The look in his eye was dangerous. Lacey knew that.

Half-charming and half-teasing. One hundred percent le-
thal. Realizing that she was powerless to resist it, she
dropped her gaze and cut into her trout again. "I wouldn't
go so far as to say that."

"Really? I thought you didn't like sex."

Her eyes snapped to his. "I never said that!"

"Oh, that's right. I believe you referred to our evening
together as a mistake."

Flustered, she picked up her wineglass and gulped a
drink. "Well, it *was* a mistake. I don't make a habit of
sleeping with a man I've only known for a few hours."

"How long do you have to know a man before you
sleep with him?"

She took another hasty sip, then another before setting
the glass down with a frown. "It isn't the length of time
that's important, it's…" she fluttered a hand helplessly.
"Well, it's…"

He rested his forearms on the table and leaned toward
her expectantly. "It's…what?" he prodded.

"I don't know," she snapped. "It's just that—well, I
don't know anything about you," she said in frustration.
Uncomfortable at the intensity with which he looked at
her, she snatched up the glass again and drank deeply.

"What would you like to know?"

She rolled her eyes. "Your name would be nice for
starters."

He chuckled and rocked his chair back on two legs and
hooked a thumb in the waist of his jeans. "You know my
name. Travis Cordell."

"Okay, then," she conceded grudgingly. "Where do
you live?"

"Houston. What else do you want to know?"

"What do you do for a living?"

He furrowed his brow. "Is that important?"

"No. I'm just curious, is all."

"Jack and I are partners in a business."

"Really?" she said, looking at him in surprise.

"Why is that so hard to believe?"

She lifted a shoulder and took another sip of her wine. "I don't know. It's just that you…"

"That I, what?"

Embarrassed, she looked away. "Well…you did have on camouflage pants when you arrived at the wedding."

"So you thought I was a soldier?"

She whipped her head around to stare at him, then sputtered a laugh when she saw the glint of teasing in his eyes. "No," she said, then sighed. "I don't know what I thought. But I certainly would've never guessed you to be a businessman."

"I'm not much of one. Jack's the brains behind the outfit." He pushed up a sleeve and bent his arm, flexing his bicep. "And I'm the muscle."

She tossed back her head and laughed fully. She wasn't sure if it was the wine or if it was Travis who was putting her so much at ease, but she suddenly realized that she was actually enjoying their conversation. She pushed aside her plate, rested her arms on the table and leaned toward him. "Tell me more."

"Like what?"

"Like what you do when you're not working."

"Fish."

She waited for him to add something more, and when he didn't, she said, "That's all? Just fish?"

"Yep. Just fish." He mimicked her posture, resting his arms on the table and leaning forward.

The table was small. Their faces close. So close she could see in the soft candlelight the squint lines that fanned from the corners of his eyes, the flecks of gold in his brown irises. He smiled and the flecks of gold danced, mesmerizing her. "You have a really nice smile," she said absently.

"Yeah, I know."

She reared back in surprise, then choked on a laugh. "And an ego the size of Texas."

"Yeah, that, too," he replied, then added with a grin, "And handsome, to boot."

Enchanted as much with him as she was by the wine and the candlelight, she leaned close again. "So why is a handsome man with a nice smile still single?"

"Who said I was?"

She jackknifed to attention, her eyes going wide in horror. "You're married?"

He tossed back his head and laughed. "No."

Huffing a breath, she balled her napkin and threw it at his face. "You jerk."

He ducked, catching the napkin before it hit him on the nose, and chuckled. "Scared you there for a minute."

"I wasn't scared," she said and snatched up her glass again. Surprised to find it empty, she reached for the bottle.

Travis snagged it before she could, then leaned to fill her glass. "Would you be disappointed if I was married?" he asked, glancing over at her as he poured the wine.

"No, I'd be mad," she replied irritably.

"Mad?" He set the bottle down and rested his arms on the table again, watching her. "Why?"

"Because I...well, because I slept with you," she finished, her cheeks flaming.

"You don't sleep with married men?"

She huffed another breath and lifted her glass. "No, I don't."

"I'm not married, so I guess that makes it all right for you sleep with me again, huh?"

"I won't *sleep* with you again because I don't *know* you," she reminded him.

"Sure you do. I just spent the last thirty minutes telling you all about me."

Lacey rolled her eyes, then, finding his logic as infuriating as it was consistent, she started laughing. "You're impossible."

"No, I'm determined."

"I've already told you that I'm not going to let you seduce me."

He stood and dropped the napkin on the table, then held out his hand to her. "If you're not going to let me seduce you, then the least you can do is dance with me."

Eyes wide, she let him pull her to her feet. "But there isn't any music!"

He tugged her toward the door. "Sure there is. Can't you hear it?" He let the door close behind them and pulled her into his arms. "Listen real close," he whispered at her ear.

Her cheek resting against his, she listened, looking over his shoulder at the sky where the moon hung like a Japanese lantern filled with golden light. After a moment, she whispered back, "I don't hear anything."

"You're not concentrating hard enough," he scolded. "Close your eyes."

Dutifully, Lacey did as instructed and waited.

"Feel that?" He flattened his hand against her back and pressed her close to his chest. "That's my heart beating for you."

He began to sway, then slowly guided her into a waltz, dancing with her beneath the full moon.

The music flowed through Lacey like wine, warming

her blood and making her light-headed. "I don't think I've ever done this before," she murmured dreamily.

"Danced?"

She smiled softly and opened her eyes, tipping her face up to look at the moon and the stars that twinkled overhead. "No," she whispered, afraid she'd break the magical spell if she spoke too loudly. "This. Dancing barefoot in the moonlight with a man I hardly know and with no music to guide our steps."

"But there is music," he insisted and spun her in a fast circle, making her laugh. He spun her back into his arms and held her close, looking down at her. "Can't you hear it?"

She stared up at him, feeling the cadence of his heart beating in rhythm with hers. "Yes," she murmured. "I can hear it." She watched his eyes darken and his smile slowly fade. Then his face was lowering to hers.

"I *am* going to seduce you," he warned.

"Too late," she whispered as his lips touched hers. "You already have."

Unable to sleep, Lacey stared out the window opposite the old iron bed. Stars glittered in the night sky like diamonds on blue-black velvet, while moonlight spilled a ribbon of gold across the field beyond. Hours before, she'd waltzed with Travis beneath that moon, snuggled against his muscled chest, the beat of their joined hearts guiding their steps.

Aware of the weight of the arm that draped her waist from behind, she hugged it tighter against her. How did he do it? she wondered in bewilderment. She hadn't wanted to make love with him again. She'd even told him up front that she wouldn't allow him to seduce her. And she'd meant every word...or, at least she had when she'd first said them.

But over the course of the evening he *had* managed to seduce her, slowly, mercilessly, until he'd reduced her to a quivering pool of need, ready to agree to anything just to have him hold her again, kiss her. Then he'd swept her up into his arms and carried her back into the cabin and to his bed and made love with her for hours.

Turning her head slightly, she glanced over her shoulder to look at him, still unable to believe that she was actually in his bed. But the proof was there behind her. Travis. His head resting beside hers on the pillow they shared, his eyes closed, his face relaxed in sleep. Careful not to wake him, she turned beneath his arm until she was lying on her side, facing him.

Handsome. Virile. Charming. Heartbreakingly romantic. She could think of a thousand adjectives to describe him, but none of them seemed to come close to explaining the emotion that swelled in her chest as she looked at him. She'd thought herself in love once, years ago, and the feelings she'd felt then closely resembled the feelings she was experiencing now.

No, she told herself firmly as panic began to nudge at her. She wasn't falling in love with Travis. For heaven's sake! She'd known him less than twenty-four hours!

Lust. That's what she was feeling. Pure lust. And no wonder, she thought, relieved to have identified the emotion. One kiss and he had the power to reduce even the most determined woman to begging.

Shifting her gaze to his mouth, she brushed a fingertip across his lips and shivered, remembering the feel of them on hers, the fire. He flinched, mumbled something in his sleep, then drew her closer to his chest, tucking her head beneath his chin and wrapping his arms around her.

Snuggling close, she felt the warmth of his body slowly seep into hers and the music of two hearts beating as one flow through her.

Lust, she told herself again, burrowing deeper. Nothing but lust. She closed her eyes and dreamed of dancing with him.

Lacey stood in the center of the round pen and slowly turned, keeping an eye on Buddy as he trotted around the perimeter of the pen. He didn't seem to favor the leg that he'd injured. There was no limp, no stiffness in his movements. The water therapy and massage Sam had prescribed were certainly doing their job.

Not wanting to push him too much, she commanded him to "Whoa," and he came to a quick stop, dust churning beneath his hooves.

"He's looking good."

Lacey turned at the sound of Sam's voice, unaware that she'd had an audience. "Thanks to you," she said, smiling her gratitude. Since she was through for the day, she crossed to her horse and clipped the lead rope to the halter, then led him toward the side of the pen where Sam waited.

Sam swung open the gate and held it while Lacey led her horse through. "I didn't do anything but make a few suggestions. You're the one who's been nursing him."

"Just the same, I'm grateful."

Sam fell into step beside Lacey and walked with her back to the barn. "Are you giving him the antibiotics I gave you?"

"Just like the doctor ordered."

"Good girl."

Once inside the building, Sam opened the stall door and

waited while Lacey led Buddy inside. "Thirsty?" she asked as Lacey rejoined her in the alleyway.

"Dry as dust."

"I'll bet Mandy's got some lemonade in the refrigerator. She usually does."

Nervously, Lacey glanced toward the main house. The thought of once more entering the house where her father had lived filled her with dread. Seeing the evidence of the life he'd led. A life that he'd chosen not to share with her.

But to refuse Sam's invitation would be rude, she knew, especially considering her half sister's kindness to her. "Sounds good to me," she said, trying to put a note of enthusiasm into her voice.

They stepped from the barn and out into the bright sunshine, walking side-by-side toward the house.

"Heard you're sharing the cabin with Jack's brother," Sam said after a moment.

Heat flooded Lacey's face. She wondered if Sam, or anyone else for that matter, suspected they were sharing the bed, as well. "Yeah, I am."

Sam opened the back door and looked at Lacey, but her eyes gave nothing away as she gestured for Lacey to enter ahead of her.

"He seems like a nice enough guy," she said as Lacey passed by her.

Mandy glanced up from the table where she was peeling vegetables as Lacey and Sam stepped into the kitchen. "Who's a nice guy?"

"Travis," Sam replied as she headed for the refrigerator, leaving Lacey standing awkwardly by the door.

Mandy waved her toward a chair. "Have a seat. He is nice," she agreed. "And isn't it amazing how much he and Jack look alike?"

Sam snorted as she set two glasses on the table then
filled them with lemonade. "They're identical twins,
Mandy. Of course they look alike." She passed Lacey a
glass and sipped from her own as she dropped down onto
the chair beside her older sister.

"I know they're twins," Mandy replied defensively,
then smiled. "But it still seems odd." She shrugged phil-
osophically as she went back to her peeling. "I guess it's
because I knew Jack first and was unaware that he had a
brother, much less a twin."

Lacey listened with growing interest. Though Travis
had told her quite a bit about himself the night before, he
hadn't said much about his family. Now she wondered
why. "Jack never mentioned to you that he had a
brother?" she asked curiously.

Mandy shook her head as she continued to peel pota-
toes. "No, but then Jack didn't talk much about his past."
She chuckled softly. "In fact, Jack rarely talked to anyone
other than Alayna."

"How did they meet?"

Sam reached to steal a raw carrot from the pan of
peeled vegetables, but jerked her hand back with a yelp
when Mandy slapped it.

With a warning look her sister's way, Mandy turned
her attention to Lacey. "Alayna hired him to do the re-
modeling on her house and ended up falling head over
heels in love with him."

"Wow," Lacey said in surprise. "Sounds as if it all
happened pretty fast."

"About a month," Sam said, then chuckled wryly.
"Although I think Alayna fell for him the first time she
saw him. It just took Jack a little longer to admit that he
loved her, too."

The first time she saw him? Lacey sank back in her

chair, thinking of Travis and the fact that she'd only known him a little more than two days. Did people really fall in love that quickly? "Only a month, huh," she said absently.

The door opened and Merideth breezed in, balancing a toddler on her hip. "Hey! I saw Sam's truck out front. Are y'all having a party and didn't invite me?" Her smile melted when her gaze met Lacey's. "I didn't know *you* were here."

"Oh, for heaven's sake, Merideth," Mandy scolded, "sit down and be nice."

Pursing her lips, Merideth plopped down in the chair next to Lacey. "I'll sit, but I don't do nice."

Sam chuckled. "You'll have to forgive Merideth," she told Lacey. "She's having a hard time accepting the fact that she's no longer the baby of the family." At Lacey's puzzled look, Sam explained, "Until you showed up, Merideth was the youngest of Lucas's daughters. Now, you hold that honor."

"If you're suggesting that I'm jealous of her," Merideth cried indignantly, "you're sorely mistaken."

"Why else would you insist on being so rude?" Sam asked pointedly.

Wide-eyed, Lacey listened to the exchange, shifting her gaze from Sam to Merideth and back to Sam, as if following the progress of a tennis match.

Mandy shoved a potato and the peeler into Sam's hands. "That's enough, you two," she scolded, standing. She leaned across the table and, smiling fondly, took the toddler from Merideth. "Y'all are going to upset Lacey. She didn't grow up with sisters and isn't accustomed to sibling rivalry, is she, sweetie pie?" she asked, turning her attention to the little girl. The toddler grabbed fistfuls of Mandy's hair and pulled until their noses were pressed together.

"Yank her bald-headed, Cassie!" Merideth and Sam yelled in unison.

Laughing, Mandy carefully unwound the child's tiny fingers from her hair. "In your dreams," she told her sisters, then turned to Lacey, still smiling. "Have you met Merideth's daughter?"

"No," Lacey said, amazed at how easily the women moved from taking potshots at each other to laughing together. "I don't think so."

"Well, it's time you did. Lacey, this is your niece Cassie Carter. Cassie, this is your aunt Lacey."

Aunt Lacey? She swallowed hard, emotion clogging her throat. She'd never been referred to as Aunt Lacey before. Without any sisters or brothers to provide the nieces and nephews required to earn the distinction, she'd never thought she would be. But now she was. And to a McCloud, no less.

While she was trying to decide what she thought about this new status, Cassie leaned toward her and held out her arms. Unsure what was expected of her, Lacey glanced at Mandy.

Mandy smiled and offered her the child. "Better watch out. She'll steal your heart."

Lacey took the toddler and held her up, letting the child plant tennis shoes no longer than Lacey's thumb on her thighs. "I don't know much about kids," she said nervously.

Mandy laughed as she sat back down and picked up another potato. "Don't worry. She won't break."

Lacey glanced from Cassie's cherubic face to Merideth. "She doesn't look anything like you," she said in surprise.

"Lucky kid," Sam muttered under her breath.

Merideth shot her sister a frown before turning back to Lacey. "That's because I'm not her biological mother."

"Oh," Lacey replied in embarrassment. "Sorry. I didn't know."

Merideth lifted a shoulder then leaned to wipe a drip of drool from Cassie's lower lip. "Cassie is John Lee's sister's baby," she explained and smiled adoringly at the child. "John Lee was given custody of her when his sister was killed in an accident almost a year ago. After we married, we adopted her."

"That must have been tough," Lacey murmured, staring at the child.

"What? John Lee taking on the responsibility of raising his niece?"

"Well, yeah," Lacey said, turning to look at Merideth. "That, too. But I was thinking more about Cassie losing her mother."

Merideth took Cassie from Lacey and tossed her high in the air, making the child squeal with delight. "Yes, it is," she said smiling sadly, then drew Cassie to her breasts and gave her a tight hug. She sat her down on her lap, then dug a toy from the bag she'd draped over the back of the chair and offered it to the child to play with. "But she'll never want for love," she added firmly, dropping a kiss on the end of Cassie's nose. "John Lee and I will see to that."

Lacey saw the devotion in Merideth's eyes, the love she obviously felt for the child, as well as her resolve to fulfill the child's needs. Regret welled in her chest. She'd never known that kind of love from a parent, biological or otherwise. And knew she never would. Feeling the sting of unexpected tears, abruptly she rose from her chair. "I'd better be going."

Mandy looked up at her in surprise. "So soon? Why don't you stick around and eat lunch with us? We're just having vegetable stew, but you're welcome to join us."

"Thanks," Lacey murmured as she headed for the door, "but I've got some things I need to do."

Instead of returning to the cabin, Lacey drove around, needing time alone to sort through the conflicting emotions that churned through her. A family in Missouri that didn't care for her. A family in Texas that she hadn't even known existed until a few days before, and who *did* seem to care for her.

How could that be?

On impulse, she whipped her truck into a service station and parked in front of a phone booth. Hopping down, she dug change from her pocket and punched in a series of numbers. Inhaling deeply, she waited through three rings before there was an answer.

"Mother, it's me, Lacey," she said into the receiver.

"Where are you?"

The response wasn't the one she'd hoped for from her mother, nor was the tone of voice with which it had been spoken. Lacey had secretly, if foolishly, yearned for some show of concern from her mother, maybe even relief that Lacey had made the call, breaking the long months of silence that stretched between them.

But, as usual, Lacey was disappointed.

"I'm in Austin," she said, plucking nervously at the phone cord. "At Lucas's ranch."

Nothing but silence followed her announcement, yet Lacey heard the disapproval in it.

"I wanted to meet him," she said, feeling as if an explanation was expected of her, though none was voiced.

"Why?" her mother snapped. "He certainly never wanted to meet you."

Though she knew what her mother said was true, hearing the bitter words stung. Lacey glanced up at the sky, blinking back tears. "He's dead, Mother."

"Lucas?"

"Yes. He died over thirteen years ago of a heart attack."

"Why are you telling me this?"

Lacey ducked her head and chipped at the loose rock on the drive as she dragged a wrist beneath her eyes. "I don't know. I guess I thought you'd want to know."

"Why? The man means nothing to me."

"I have three half sisters," Lacey murmured.

"I know."

Lacey snapped up her head, her fingers tightening on the receiver. "You knew, and you never told me?"

"Why should I? He wanted them, not you."

The malicious stab hit its target, as intended, taking another chunk out of Lacey's already battered heart.

"They're McClouds," her mother continued bitterly. "Vicious and selfish and mean."

"I'm a McCloud, too," Lacey reminded her.

Again, silence roared in her ear.

Knowing that trying to explain her feelings to her mother was useless, with a sigh, Lacey changed the subject. "Buddy's hurt."

"What happened?"

Once more, Lacey searched for concern in her mother's voice, but found none. She squeezed her forehead between the width of her hand and fought back tears of disappointment. "He spooked while I was trying to load him and cut his shoulder on the trailer door."

"Well, there goes your chance at the national title."

"Maybe," Lacey replied stubbornly, hearing the smug pleasure in her mother's voice. "Maybe not."

"Well, you certainly can't hope to win if you don't have a horse to compete on."

Lacey glanced in the direction of the highway as an eighteen-wheeler roared by. "We'll compete again," she said with conviction, watching the truck disappear. "Sam's taking care of him."

"Sam?"

"One of Lucas's daughters. She's a vet."

"Oh."

She heard the disapproval in her mother's clipped response and decided to tell it all. "I'm staying at a cabin on their ranch."

"Whose ranch?"

"Lucas's. Or, rather, his daughters'. He left it to them."

"The three he *claimed,*" her mother clarified spitefully, "not the four he *sired.*"

"I don't want a part of his ranch," Lacey returned angrily. "That's not why I came here."

"Then you're a bigger fool than I thought. You ought to hire yourself a lawyer and demand your share of his estate. Or better yet, perhaps I should."

"I don't want anything that was his. Can't you understand that?"

"Then why did you go there?" her mother shouted furiously.

Tears welled in Lacey's eyes. "Because I wanted to meet him. Because I needed to know why he didn't want me."

"And did you find out why?" her mother shot back.

Weary from arguing with her mother, Lacey braced her forearm against the wall of the phone booth and rested her forehead on it. "No. Lucas is the only one who can answer that question, and he's dead."

Five

———

Bare chested, Travis sat on the ridge of the barn's roof, sipping a cold beer while watching for another glimpse of Lacey. She'd returned a couple of hours before, after caring for her horse, and had pulled her truck and trailer under one of the trees close to the cabin. She had been inside the trailer ever since. Every once in a while, he'd see her push open the door that led to the sleeping quarters and pitch an armload of debris outside, then disappear inside again.

The woman was a firehouse of motion. He chuckled, wondering what was fueling this sudden burst of energy. He'd think she'd be exhausted after the night they'd spent trying to wear out the springs on that old iron bed. Hell, he knew he was.

He watched the door open again, but this time, instead of throwing something out, she hopped to the ground. She

paused a moment, lifting her arms above her head and
bowing her back as she stretched.

Mmm-mmm, he thought as he watched her breasts
strain against her shirt's fabric. What a sight. Made him
hungry for another taste of her, and he had been sure that
he'd more than satisfied that particular hankering the night
before.

While he continued to watch from his perch on the
barn's roof, she dropped her arms and headed for her
pickup. She dug around inside a moment, then headed
back for the trailer, her arms loaded down with tools.

He rubbed the icy can thoughtfully across his chest,
cooling his heated skin, and wondered again what was
behind this sudden burst of energy.

There's only one way to find out, Cordell, he told himself and pushed himself to his feet. Go and see.

Once on the ground, he fished another couple of beers
from the cooler he'd stashed just inside the barn, then
headed for the trailer. With his hands full, he rapped his
elbow against the side of the trailer. "Lacey? Open up."

"What do you want?"

Surprised by the unfriendly greeting, he peered through
the screen, but could see nothing but her shadowed form
on the other side. He lifted the beers in invitation.
"Thought you might like something cold to drink."

When she didn't move to open the door, he dropped
his arms in frustration. "Dang it, Lacey! Are you going
to invite me in, or am I going to have to drink these beers
myself?"

She pushed open the door, though he could see that she
did so reluctantly.

"I guess I could take a break for a few minutes."

He quickly stepped into the trailer before she could
change her mind. "About time," he muttered and shoved

a beer in her hand. "I was melting out there." It took a moment for his eyes to adjust to the change in light, and when they did, he glanced her way and saw her red-rimmed eyes. He took a step toward her and peered more closely. "Hey," he said in concern, brushing his knuckles across her cheek. "Have you been crying?"

She jerked away from his touch and turned her back to him.

Stunned, Travis stared. He knew that Lacey was a private person, one who preferred to do her crying alone. Their first night together in the cabin had taught him that. With anyone else, he would've honored that need for privacy and gone about his own business. But, for some reason, with Lacey, he discovered he couldn't. Not when he saw the way her fingers were trembling as she tried to open the can of beer.

He took the can from her, popped the top and handed it back to her. "Did your horse take a turn for the worse?" he asked, watching her closely.

"No," she replied and sniffed. "He's fine."

He stepped closer and laid a hand on her shoulder. "Then, what's wrong?"

"Nothing." She stepped from beneath his hand and took a sip of her beer.

Travis was sure that something had happened to make her cry, and feared—judging by the way she kept dodging physical contact with him—that the "something" had to do with him and the fact that he'd succeeded in seducing her the night before.

He glanced around, looking for an excuse to hang around until he could determine the reason for her tears. "You've been busy," he said, noting that she'd ripped the chipped linoleum from the floor, exposing the metal floor below. A sink lay on its side on the floor and joints of PVC pipe lay scattered around it like the pieces of a jigsaw puzzle.

"Some," she replied indifferently.

"Having trouble with the plumbing?" he asked, pushing the toe of his boot against the tangle of pipe on the floor.

She wiped the back of her hand across her mouth, removing the moisture left there from the can. "A little."

"Need some help?"

She glanced at him, then away again. "I can handle it."

Refusing to let her indifference sway him from his determination to stay, he squatted down and sifted through the pipe. He set his beer aside and picked up the sink, then stood and dropped it into place over the hole cut in the narrow counter. He squatted down again and picked up a piece of pipe. He held it up to the light spilling through the high window above the bench, and twisted it around, examining it. "Do you have a crescent wrench?"

Though he could tell that she didn't want his help, she set her beer aside and knelt on the floor, rummaging through the tools piled there. Finding the requested wrench, she handed it to him. He made sure his fingers brushed hers in the exchange, and was rewarded when her gaze snapped to his at the contact. He rubbed his thumb along her knuckles and saw the heat flare in her eyes before she jerked her hand from his.

The action proved to him that she wasn't as unaffected by his touch as she wanted to pretend...and convinced him that her tears were ones of regret because she'd allowed him to seduce her again. And that bothered Travis. He didn't like being the cause of anyone's misery, least of all Lacey's. She had enough people in her life causing her grief.

He picked up a piece of pipe, and placed the wrench around it, adjusting the size of the clamp. "I think I was twelve when I installed my first sink."

"Twelve?"

Relieved to hear a response from her, he kept his gaze focused on the two joints of pipe he was fitting together. "Yep. My daddy was a builder, and in the summertime he would take Jack and me out on the job with him." He glanced her way. "Got any sealant?"

She quickly produced a can, then sat back and watched as he painted the sealant on the joint.

"He taught us everything he knew about the business. Jack took to the building trade like a duck to water. But me—" he chuckled, shaking his head as he remembered those early years "—well, let's just say I was a disappointment to our old man."

Lacey knew all about being a disappointment. Without meaning to, or even knowing why, she was a constant disappointment to her parents. Surprised to learn that she and Travis had that in common, she inched closer. "Why? Because you didn't share his love for building?"

Sensing that she was letting her guard down, if only a little, Travis stuck his head up under the cupboard to inspect the connections. "Oh, I liked the building trade just fine." He rolled to his back inside the narrow space, then lifted his head to look at her. He shot her a wink. "I just liked fishing better." Grinning, he stretched out a hand. "Hand me that crescent."

Lacey passed him the wrench, then scooted closer, watching as he fitted the pipe into place and secured it. She passed him the sealant, anticipating his need for it. "Are you and your family close?"

"Used to be." He grunted, the muscles of his arms straining as he tightened the fittings.

"What happened?"

He balanced the wrench on his chest and reached for another piece of pipe. Lacey snagged it and pressed it into his hand. With a mumbled thanks, he joined the pipe to the others.

"What happened?" she asked again, unable to contain her curiosity.

"You don't want to know."

She frowned at him. "I asked, didn't I?"

He lifted his head again, but this time he wasn't smiling. His eyes were flat, emotionless, as he met her gaze. "I committed the unforgivable sin." He dropped his head back down and plucked the wrench from his chest. Setting his jaw, he put all his muscle behind the tool.

Lacey watched him fit another piece of pipe into place, her mind reeling with all the possibilities. The unforgivable sin? The only sin she could think of that was so bad as to be unforgivable was murder...and judging by the look on Travis's face at the moment, she wasn't so sure he wasn't capable of it. "Did you kill somebody?" The question was out before she even realized she intended to ask it.

He lifted his head, then snorted a laugh when he saw the fear in her expression. "No, I didn't kill anybody," he replied dryly. He lowered his head and gritted his teeth as he put the final turn on the wrench. Dropping the tool to his chest, he lifted his head again, and met her gaze. "What about you? Are you close to your family?"

She rolled her eyes. "Hardly."

"Why not?"

She hesitated a moment, tempted to tell him about the conversation she'd had earlier with her mother and how much her mother's words had hurt...then quickly decided she didn't want to think about her mother any more. When she did, it always made her mad or sad, and she didn't want to be either. Not anymore. Angling her head at a cocky angle, she said instead, "I committed the unforgivable sin."

Chuckling, Travis scooted from underneath the sink, and sat up. "You too, huh?"

Lacey nodded, smiling. "Yep. Me, too."

Lifting a hip, he pulled a rag from his back pocket and wiped the sealant from his fingers. "You aren't upset about last night, are you?"

Confused, she peered at him. "Last night?"

"Yeah," he said, keeping his gaze on his hands as he cleaned them. "You know, about me seducing you."

Her heart melted a little as she stared at him, realizing his concern. "No. I'm not upset." His relief was so obvious, that Lacey had to laugh. "But I am curious as to how you managed to seduce me. I was determined you weren't going to, you know."

"Yeah, I know." He lifted his hip to replace the rag and grinned at her. "It's my charm. Women find it irresistible." He stood and offered her his hand. "Wanna play hooky?"

Lacey looked around at the work still to be done, then back up at him and arched a brow. "What did you have in mind?"

"Ever been fishing?"

"No," she said, then shuddered, remembering the smelly fish he had cleaned in the cabin's kitchen sink.

He took her by the hand, curling his fingers around hers. "Then you're in for a real treat," he said and tugged her toward the door.

Lacey lay with her back resting against the rowboat's bow, her eyes closed and her legs stretched out, trying to convince herself she wasn't seasick. She dropped a hand over the side of the boat and dipped her fingers in the water, then dribbled the moisture onto her face. "And this is what you call heaven?" she asked doubtfully.

Travis glanced over at her before drawing his rod back over his shoulder and casting again. "Close as I'll probably ever come." He watched his fly strike the water about fifty feet away, then dip beneath the surface.

"Do you fish very often?"

"Every chance I get." He began to slowly turn the crank on his reel, watching the fly skip along the lake's surface as he drew in his line. "In fact, I was on a fishing trip in Mexico when I got the message from Jack telling me he was getting married."

"And you cut your trip short, just to keep your brother from making the biggest mistake of his life, right?"

He heard the sarcasm in her voice, and glanced her way and found her smiling at him. "The *second* biggest mistake," he clarified, then winked at her before turning his attention back to his line. "And it was a hardship, I assure you."

Careful not to rock the boat, Lacey sat up, then wound her hair up in a knot, holding it on top of her head. "What was his first big mistake?"

"Marrying the first time around."

She looked around, searching for something to hold her hair in place. "What is it with you? Do you have something against marriage?"

"Not as long as it's not *me* doing the marrying."

"*Or* Jack," she reminded him and pushed the plastic stick she'd found in his tackle box into the knot of her hair.

"I don't have a problem with Jack getting married."

She looked up at him in surprise, then laughed. "*This*

from the man who staged a brawl while trying to stop his brother's wedding?''

He frowned at the reminder. "I didn't set out to start a brawl." He turned his gaze on the lake again, watching his line as he slowly reeled it in. "But I had to be sure he wasn't making a mistake."

"And you've decided he wasn't?"

"I don't know, yet."

"They're due home soon, aren't they?"

"Yeah, tomorrow."

"So you'll talk to him then and put your mind at ease?"

"Yeah, I suppose."

"If you decide he's not making another mistake, will you go back to Houston?"

He glanced over at her. "Trying to get rid of me already?"

She blushed. "No, I was just curious."

He leaned over, caught the end of his line and drew it into the boat. After unhooking his fly, he tucked it into his tackle box, then selected another one. "Are you going to miss me?"

The question came out of nowhere and caught Lacey totally off-guard. She hadn't thought about Travis leaving, or herself either, for that matter, and now that she was forced to, she felt an unexpected sense of loss.

Though at first she had worked hard at disliking him, over the last three days she'd grown rather attached to him. Sleeping curled in his arms. Waking up next to him. Laughing with him. Dancing with him beneath the moon. He'd added something to her life that was missing before. Something that she hadn't even known was lacking until she'd met him. Joy. A sense of the outrageous. Companionship.

She was relieved that he was concentrating on attaching the fly to the line and not looking at her when he posed the question, because it gave her a moment to school her features and force a cocky smile. "Miss you? What's to miss?"

He glanced over at her and waggled a brow. "Want me to show you?"

She huffed a laugh and rolled her eyes. "There goes that ego of yours again," she said dryly.

He laid his rod and reel down and hopped over the seat that separated them. "No brag, ma'am. Just fact."

The boat pitched wildly at his movement, and Lacey clamped her hands over the gunwales and held on for dear life. "Travis!" she squealed. "Stop!"

His smile widened as he reached for the waist of his jeans. "What's the matter, Lacey? Afraid you won't be able to bear seeing all you're going to miss?"

She tightened her hands on the gunwales and swallowed hard, watching as he unfastened the first button on his jeans, then the next. Without warning, he dropped his pants to his ankles. Her eyes went wide, then snapped to his. "Travis!" She looked wildly about, sure that someone could see him. "For heaven's sake! It's broad daylight!"

"We're in no-man's land," he said, laughing. "There isn't a soul within miles of this lake." He lifted a leg to pull the jeans over his bare foot and the boat pitched wildly.

Lacey's stomach rolled right along with it. Clinging to the boat with one hand, she pressed the other against her middle and squeezed her eyes shut. "Travis, please," she moaned pitifully. "You're making me sick."

She heard a thump, then his knees bumped hers.

"Man, you really know how to hurt a guy," he said, sounding wounded.

She opened her eyes to see that he was sitting on the seat opposite her. Thankful that at last the boat had stilled, she exhaled a long, shaky breath. "I'm sorry, but I was getting seasick."

"Seasick!" he echoed, then tossed back his head and laughed. "Lacey, this is nothing but a big pond."

"The motion's the same," she said, and swallowed back the nausea that rose just thinking about it.

He eased from the seat and dropped to his knees in front of her. "Ever made love on a waterbed?"

At his movement, the boat rocked from side to side, and she sucked in a breath and grabbed for the gunwales again. Frantically, she shook her head. "No, and please be still."

His gaze on hers, he closed his hands over hers and slowly uncurled her stiff fingers from the sides of the boat. "The boat's not going to turn over," he said gently.

"How can you be sure?" she asked, her eyes round with fear.

"Because I just know."

Without the boat to hold on to any longer, she wrapped her fingers around his and clung. "If you're not going to fish anymore, can we go back to shore?" she asked hopefully.

"I have a better idea." He leaned forward, blocking the sun from her face, and closed his mouth over hers. He sipped slowly, then traced her lips with his tongue. "Let's make love."

"Here?" she asked weakly, forcing open heavy-lidded eyes to look at him.

"Yeah. Here."

"But—"

He closed his mouth over hers again and thrust his tongue deeply into her mouth, sending shivers of anticipation skating down her spine. Tugging her hands from his, she flung them around his neck and clung. "All right," she said breathlessly, then pressed her lips against his again. "But try not to move around too much, okay?"

Laughing, Travis pulled her onto his lap.

Their arms wound around each other's waists, Travis and Lacey stepped from the shadow of the woods, laughing like loons.

Merideth, Mandy and Sam watched their approach from the front porch of the cabin.

"What do you suppose they've been up to?" Mandy whispered, watching the two stumble their way, laughing, toward the cabin.

Merideth chuckled softly. "A little hanky-panky would be my guess."

"No way," Sam said emphatically. "They hardly know each other."

"You're such an innocent," Merideth said in exasperation, then chuckled. "Look," she said, giving Mandy a nudge. "Her shirt's buttoned up all wrong."

"At least she's wearing one," Mandy replied, her eyes focused on Travis's bare chest.

Merideth shifted her gaze slightly and whistled low under her breath. "What a body," she murmured appreciatively.

Sam huffed a breath. "You two are sick, you know it? Spying on them like some kind of voyeurs or something." She stepped from the shadow of the porch, and shouted, "Hey, Lacey! Travis! You've got company!"

"Spoilsport," Merideth muttered under her breath as she stepped up beside her sister, then smiled and waved